The Whistling Schoolboy

Ruskin Bond has been writing for over sixty years, and has now over 120 titles in print—novels, collections of stories, poetry, essays, anthologies and books for children. His first novel, *The Room on the Roof*, received the prestigious John Llewellyn Rhys Award in 1957. He has also received the Padma Shri (1999), the Padma Bhushan (2014) and two awards from the Sahitya Akademi—one for his short stories and another for his writings for children. In 2012, the Delhi government gave him its Lifetime Achievement Award.

Born in 1934, Ruskin Bond grew up in Jamnagar, Shimla, New Delhi and Dehradun. Apart from three years in the UK, he has spent all his life in India, and now lives in Mussoorie with his adopted family.

A shy person, Ruskin says he likes being a writer because 'When I'm writing there's nobody watching me. Today, it's hard to find a profession where you're not being watched!'

The Whistling Schoolboy
and other stories of school life

RUSKIN BOND

RED TURTLE
RUPA

Published in Red Turtle by
Rupa Publications India Pvt. Ltd 2015
7/16, Ansari Road, Daryaganj
New Delhi 110002

Sales centres:
Allahabad Bengaluru Chennai
Hyderabad Jaipur Kathmandu
Kolkata Mumbai

Copyright © Ruskin Bond 2015

All rights reserved.
No part of this publication may be reproduced, transmitted, or stored in a retrieval system, in any form or by any means, electronic, mechanical, photocopying, recording or otherwise, without the prior permission of the publisher.

This is a work of fiction. Names, characters, places and incidents are either the product of the author's imagination or are used fictitiously and any resemblance to any actual person, living or dead, events or locales is entirely coincidental.

ISBN: 978-81-291-3579-7

Eighth impression 2018

10 9 8

The moral right of the author has been asserted.

Printed at Parksons Graphics Pvt. Ltd, Mumbai

This book is sold subject to the condition that it shall not, by way of trade or otherwise, be lent, resold, hired out, or otherwise circulated, without the publisher's prior consent, in any form of binding or cover other than that in which it is published.

Contents

Introduction vii

SCHOOL DAYS WITH RUSKIN
The Four Feathers 3
Be Prepared 11
My Desert Island 17
Remember This Day 25
Letter to My Father 30
Our Great Escape 36
Reading Was My Religion 46

SCHOOL DAYS, RULE DAYS
Here Comes Mr Oliver 55
The Lady in White 63
Missing Person: H.M. 67

Miss Babcock's Big Toe	71
A Dreadful Gurgle	75
A Face in the Dark	79
The Whistling Schoolboy	83
Children of India	92
The School among the Pines	100

Introduction

Did I read school stories when I was at school?

Very seldom; caught up in the monotonous routine of boarding-school life, I preferred to read about faraway places, desert islands, pirates, jungles infested with tigers and crocodiles—anything as far removed as possible from classroom and dormitories!

I did, however, have one literary boy-hero. He was William Brown ('Just William' to his thousands of fans), who did everything possible to stay out of school. If he did turn up, he was usually late. And if he remained in school till the end of the day, his headmaster would have a nervous breakdown.

William is a little out of fashion now. Rebellious schoolboys are unwelcome in a technologically advanced, moralistic, exam-oriented society. We prefer a polished Bill Gates to an eccentric Einstein. Eccentrics

INTRODUCTION

do unpredictable things, and we have become afraid of the unpredictable.

We had exams in my schooldays too, but they were only a part of the process of growing up. There were also such things as nature walks and picnics, excursions to historical places, football games, cricket, comic books, visits to the cinema, ice cream parlours and clandestine visits to the neighbouring girls' school.

Some of these things I remember, and some I have written about. Here is a personal selection. Dip into it, enjoy meeting some unusual people, and then back to your fantasy world!

Ruskin Bond

School Days with Ruskin

The Four Feathers

Our school dormitory was a very long room with about thirty beds, fifteen on either side of the room. This was good for pillow fights. Class V would take on Class VI (the two senior classes in our Prep school) and there would be plenty of space for leaping, struggling small boys, pillows flying, feathers flying, until there was a cry of 'Here comes Fishy!' or 'Here comes Olly!' and either Mr Fisher, the Headmaster, or Mr Oliver, the Senior Master, would come striding in, cane in hand, to put an end to the general mayhem. Pillow fights were allowed, up to a point; nobody got hurt. But parents sometimes complained if, at the end of the term, a boy came home with a pillow devoid of cotton-wool or feathers.

In that last year at Prep school in Shimla, there were

four of us who were close friends—Bimal, whose home was in Bombay; Riaz, who came from Lahore; Bran, who hailed from Vellore; and your narrator, who lived wherever his father (then in the Air Force) was posted.

We called ourselves the 'Four Feathers', the feathers signifying that we were companions in adventure, comrades-in-arms, and knights of the round table. Bimal adopted a peacock's feather as his emblem—he was always a bit showy. Riaz chose a falcon's feather—although we couldn't find one. Bran and I were at first offered crows or murghi feathers, but we protested vigorously and threatened a walkout. Finally, I settled for a parrot's feather (taken from Mrs Fisher's pet parrot), and Bran found a woodpecker's, which suited him, as he was always knocking things about.

Bimal was all thin legs and arms, so light and frisky that at times he seemed to be walking on air. We called him 'Bambi', after the delicate little deer in the Disney film. Riaz, on the other hand, was a sturdy boy, good at games though not very studious; but always good-natured, always smiling.

Bran was a dark, good-looking boy from the South; he was just a little spoilt—hated being given out in a cricket match and would refuse to leave the crease!—

but he was affectionate and a loyal friend. I was the 'scribe'—good at inventing stories in order to get out of scrapes—but hopeless at sums, my highest marks being twenty-two out of one hundred.

On Sunday afternoons, when there were no classes or organized games, we were allowed to roam about on the hillside below the school. The Four Feathers would laze about on the short summer grass, sharing the occasional food parcel from home, reading comics (sometimes a book), and making plans for the long winter holidays. My father, who collected everything from stamps to seashells to butterflies, had given me a butterfly net and urged me to try and catch a rare species which, he said, was found only near Chotta Shimla. He described it as a large purple butterfly with yellow and black borders on its wings. A Purple Emperor, I think it was called. As I wasn't very good at identifying butterflies, I would chase anything that happened to flit across the school grounds, usually ending up with Common Red Admirals, Clouded Yellows, or Cabbage Whites. But that Purple Emperor—that rare specimen being sought by collectors the world over—proved elusive. I would have to seek my fortune in some other line of endeavour.

One day, scrambling about among the rocks, and thorny bushes below the school, I almost fell over a small bundle lying in the shade of a young spruce tree. On taking a closer look, I discovered that the bundle was really a baby, wrapped up in a tattered old blanket.

'Feathers, feathers!' I called, 'come here and look. A baby's been left here!'

The feathers joined me and we all stared down at the infant, who was fast asleep.

'Who would leave a baby on the hillside?' asked Bimal of no one in particular.

'Someone who doesn't want it,' said Bran.

'And hoped some good people would come along and keep it,' said Riaz.

'A panther might have come along instead,' I said. 'Can't leave it here.'

'Well, we'll just have to adopt it,' said Bimal.

'We can't adopt a baby,' said Bran.

'Why not?'

'We have to be married.'

'We don't.'

'Not us, you dope. The grown-ups who adopt babies.'

Well, we can't just leave it here for grown-ups to come along,' I said.

THE FOUR FEATHERS

'We don't even know if it's a boy or a girl,' said Riaz.

'Makes no difference. A baby's a baby. Let's take it back to school.'

'And keep it in the dormitory?'

'Of course not. Who's going to feed it? Babies need milk. We'll hand it over to Mrs Fisher. She doesn't have a baby.'

'Maybe she doesn't want one. Look, it's beginning to cry. Let's hurry!'

Riaz picked up the wide-awake and crying baby and gave it to Bimal who gave it to Bran who gave it to me. The Four Feathers marched up the hill to school with a very noisy baby.

'Now it's done potty in the blanket,' I complained. 'And some of it's on my shirt.'

'Never mind,' said Bimal. 'It's in a good cause. You're a Boy Scout, remember? You're supposed to help people in distress.'

The headmaster and his wife were in their drawing room, enjoying their afternoon tea and cakes. We trudged in, and Bimal announced, 'We've got something for Mrs Fisher.'

Mrs Fisher took one look at the bundle in my arms and let out a shriek. 'What have you brought here, Bond?'

'A baby, ma'am. I think it's a girl. Do you want to adopt it?'

Mrs Fisher threw up her arms in consternation, and turned to her husband. 'What are we to do, Frank? These boys are impossible. They've picked up someone's child!'

'We'll have to inform the police,' said Mr Fisher, reaching for the telephone. 'We can't have lost babies in the school.'

Just then there was a commotion outside, and a wild-eyed woman, her clothes dishevelled, entered at the front door accompanied by several menfolk from one of the villages. She ran towards us, crying out, 'My baby, my baby! Mera bachcha! You've stolen my baby!'

'We found it on the hillside,' I stammered. 'That's right,' said Bran. 'Finder's keepers!'

'Quiet, Adams,' said Mr Fisher, holding up his hand for order and addressing the villagers in a friendly manner. 'These boys found the baby alone on the hillside and brought it here before…before…'

'Before the hyenas got it,' I put in.

'Quite right, Bond. And why did you leave your child alone?' he asked the woman.

'I put her down for five minutes so that I could

climb the plum tree and collect the plums. When I came down, the baby had gone! But I could hear it crying up on the hill. I called the menfolk and we come looking for it.'

'Well, here's your baby,' I said, thrusting it into her arms. By then I was glad to be rid of it! 'Look after it properly in future.'

'Kidnapper!' she screamed at me.

Mr Fisher succeeded in mollifying the villagers. 'These boys are good Scouts,' he told them. 'It's their business to help people.'

'Scout Law Number Three, sir,' I added. 'To be useful and helpful.'

And then the Headmaster turned the tables on the villagers. 'By the way, those plum trees belong to the school. So do the peaches and apricots. Now I know why they've been disappearing so fast!'

The villagers, a little chastened, went their way.

Mr Fisher reached for his cane. From the way he fondled it I knew he was itching to use it on our bottoms.

'No, Frank,' said Mrs Fisher, intervening on our behalf. 'It was really very sweet of them to look after that baby. And look at Bond—he's got baby-goo all over his clothes.'

'So he has. Go and take a bath, all of you. And what are you grinning about, Bond?'

'Scout Law Number Eight, sir. A Scout smiles and whistles under all difficulties.'

And so ended the first adventure of the Four Feathers.

Be Prepared

I was a Boy Scout once, although I couldn't tell a slip knot from a granny knot, nor a reef knot from a thief knot. I did know that a thief knot was to be used to tie up a thief, should you happen to catch one. I have never caught a thief—and wouldn't know what to do with one since I can't tie the right knot. I'd just let him go with a warning, I suppose. And tell him to become a Boy Scout.

'Be prepared!' That's the Boy Scout motto. And it is a good one, too. But I never seem to be well prepared for anything, be it an exam or a journey or the roof blowing off my room. I get halfway through a speech and then forget what I have to say next. Or I make a new suit to attend a friend's wedding, and then turn up in my pyjamas.

So, how did I, the most impractical of boys, survive as a Boy Scout?

Well, it seems a rumour had gone around the junior school (I was still a junior then) that I was a good cook. I had never cooked anything in my life, but of course I had spent a lot of time in the tuck shop making suggestions and advising Chimpu, who ran the tuck shop, and encouraging him to make more and better samosas, jalebies, tikkees and pakoras. For my unwanted advice, he would favour me with an occasional free samosa. So, naturally, I looked upon him as a friend and benefactor. With this qualification, I was given a cookery badge and put in charge of our troop's supply of rations.

There were about twenty of us in our troop. During the summer break our Scoutmaster, Mr Oliver, took us on a camping expedition to Taradevi, a temple-crowned mountain a few miles outside Shimla. That first night we were put to work, peeling potatoes, skinning onions, shelling peas and pounding masalas. These various ingredients being ready, I was asked, as the troop cookery expert, what should be done with them.

'Put everything in that big degchi,' I ordered. 'Pour half a tin of ghee over the lot. Add some nettle leaves, and cook for half an hour.'

When this was done, everyone had a taste, but the general opinion was that the dish lacked something. 'More salt,' I suggested.

More salt was added. It still lacked something. 'Add a cup of sugar,' I ordered.

Sugar was added to the concoction, but it still lacked something.

'We forgot to add tomatoes,' said one of the Scouts. 'Never mind,' I said. 'We have tomato sauce. Add a bottle of tomato sauce!'

'How about some vinegar?' suggested another boy. 'Just the thing,' I said. 'Add a cup of vinegar!'

'Now it's too sour,' said one of the tasters.

'What jam did we bring?' I asked.

'Gooseberry jam.'

'Just the thing. Empty the bottle!'

The dish was a great success. Everyone enjoyed it, including Mr Oliver, who had no idea what had gone into it.

'What's this called?' he asked.

'It's an all-Indian sweet-and-sour jam-potato curry,' I ventured.

'For short, just call it Bond bhujjia,' said one of the

boys. I had earned my cookery badge!

Poor Mr Oliver; he wasn't really cut out to be a Scoutmaster, any more than I was meant to be a Scout.

The following day, he told us he would give us a lesson in tracking. Taking a half-hour start, he walked into the forest, leaving behind him a trail of broken twigs, chicken feathers, pine cones and chestnuts. We were to follow the trail until we found him.

Unfortunately, we were not very good trackers. We did follow Mr Oliver's trail some way into the forest, but then we were distracted by a pool of clear water. It looked very inviting. Abandoning our uniforms, we jumped into the pool and had a great time romping about or just lying on its grassy banks and enjoying the sunshine. Many hours later, feeling hungry, we returned to our campsite and set about preparing the evening meal. It was Bond bhujjia again, but with a few variations.

It was growing dark, and we were beginning to worry about Mr Oliver's whereabouts when he limped into the camp, assisted by a couple of local villagers. Having waited for us at the far end of the forest for a couple of hours, he had decided to return by following his own trail, but in the gathering gloom he was soon lost. Village folk returning home from the temple took charge and escorted him back to the camp. He was very angry and made us return all our good-conduct and other badges, which he stuffed into his haversack. I had to give up my cookery badge.

An hour later, when we were all preparing to get into our sleeping bags for the night, Mr Oliver called out, 'Where's dinner?'

'We've had ours,' said one of the boys. 'Everything is finished, sir.'

'Where's Bond? He's supposed to be the cook. Bond, get up and make me an omelette.'

'I can't, sir.'

'Why not?'

'You have my badge. Not allowed to cook without it. Scout rule, sir.'

'I've never heard of such a rule. But you can take your badges, all of you. We return to school tomorrow.'

Mr Oliver returned to his tent in a huff.

But I relented and made him a grand omelette, garnishing it with dandelion leaves and a chilli.

'Never had such an omelette before,' confessed Mr Oliver.

'Would you like another, sir?'

'Tomorrow, Bond, tomorrow. We'll breakfast early tomorrow.'

But we had to break up our camp before we could do that because in the early hours of the next morning, a bear strayed into our camp, entered the tent where our stores were kept, and created havoc with all our provisions, even rolling our biggest degchi down the hillside.

In the confusion and uproar that followed, the bear entered Mr Oliver's tent (our Scoutmaster was already outside, fortunately) and came out entangled in his dressing gown. It then made off towards the forest, a comical sight in its borrowed clothes.

And though we were a troop of brave little scouts, we thought it better to let the bear keep the gown.

My Desert Island

Although I was a good football goalkeeper (not too much running around), I found most games rather boring. Cricket was one of them. Especially, when one had to turn up at the 'nets' in order to bowl endless overs at an important player who was there simply to practise his shots. And then to sit around for the better part of the day, waiting for a chance to bat, and then to be given out LBW (Leg before Wicket) by an umpire (i.e., teacher) who hated you anyway and was just waiting for a chance to get even…and so, before we went out to field, or in the process of running after a ball that refused to slow down, I would get a cramp in one of my legs (sometimes genuine) and leave the field, retiring to the dormitory where I would enjoy an hour or two of refreshing sleep while the rest of the team slipped and stumbled about on the stony outfield.

No grass in our school 'flats' or playing fields. As a goalkeeper, I lost a considerable amount of skin from my knees and elbows; even so, it was better than chasing cricket balls.

Elsewhere, I think I have mentioned my antipathy to running races. Why bother to come first when, with less effort, you can come in last and be none the worse for it? There is no law against coming in last. Those marathon runs took us through the town's outskirts, and along the way were numerous vendors selling roasted corn, or peanuts, or hot pakoras. Those of us who were not desirous of winning medals (they were made of tin, anyway) would stop for refreshment (making sure the teacher on duty was out of sight) and bring up the rear of the race while the poor winner, looking famished and quite exhausted, would have to wait patiently for the school dinner—usually rubbery chapattis and a curry made of undercooked potatoes and stringy 'French' beans: more string than beans.

Running wasn't my forte, but I wasn't too bad at the shot-put, and could throw that iron ball a considerable distance. The teacher who had been our cricket coach and umpire made the mistake of standing too close to

MY DESERT ISLAND

me, and I dropped the shot (quite accidentally) on his toes, rendering him unfit for duty for a few days.

'Sorry, sir!' I said. 'It slipped.'

But he wasn't the forgiving type; when the boxing tournaments came around, he put me in the ring with the school's 'most scientific' boxer. Not being of a scientific bent, I threw science to the winds and used my famous headbutt to good effect. Why box for three rounds when everything can be settled in one?

Games were, of course, compulsory in most boarding schools. They were supposed to turn you into real men, even if your IQ remained at zero.

This commitment to the values of the playing fields of Eton and Rugby meant that literature came very low on that list of the school's priorities. We had a decent enough library, consisting mainly of books that had been gifted to the school; but as reading them wasn't compulsory (as opposed to boxing and cricket), the library was an island seldom inhabited except by one shipwrecked and literary young man—yours truly.

My housemaster, Mr Brown, realizing that I was a bookish boy, had the wisdom to put me in charge of the library. This meant that I had access to the keys, and that I could visit that storeroom of books whenever I liked.

The Great Escape!

And so, whenever I could dodge cricket nets or PT (physical training), or swimming lessons, or extra classes of any kind, I would ship away to my desert island and there, surrounded by books in lieu of coconut palms, read or write or dawdle or dream, secure in the knowledge that no one was going to disturb me, since no one else was interested in reading books.

Today, teachers and parents and the world at large complain that the reading habit is dying out, that youngsters don't read, that no one wants books. Well, all I can say is that they never did! If reading is a minority pastime today it was even more so sixty years ago. And there was no television then, no Internet, no Facebook, no tweeting and twittering, no video games, no DVD players, none of the distractions that we blame today for the decline in the reading habit.

In truth, it hasn't declined. I keep meeting young people who read, and many who want to write. This was not the case when I was a boy. If I was asked what I wanted to do after school, and I said, 'I'm going to be a writer,' everyone would laugh. Writers were eccentric

MY DESERT ISLAND

creatures who lived on the moon or in some never-never land; they weren't real. So I stopped saying I was going to be a writer and instead said I was going to be a detective. Somehow, that made better sense. After all, Dick Tracy was a comic-book hero. And there was a radio series featuring Bulldog Drummond, a precursor to James Bond.

In the library, I soon had many good friends—Dickens and Chekhov and Maupassant and Barrie and Somerset Maugham and Hugh Walpole and P.G. Wodehouse and many others, and even Bulldog Drummond, whose adventures were set forth by 'Sapper', whose real name was H.C. McNeile.

Pseudonyms were popular once. 'Saki' was H.H. Munro. 'O. Henry' was William Porter. 'Mark Twain' was Samuel Clemens. 'Ellery Queen' was two people.

My own favourite was 'A Modern Sinbad', who wrote some wonderful sea stories—*Spin a Yarn Sailor* (1934), a battered copy still treasured by me, full of great storms and colourful ships' captains, and sailors singing shanties; but I have never been able to discover his real name, and his few books are hard to find. Perhaps one of my young computer-friendly readers can help!

Apart from Tagore, there were very few Indian

authors writing in English in the 1940s. R.K. Narayan's first book was introduced to the world by Graham Greene, Mulk Raj Anand's by E.M. Forster; they were followed in the fifties by Raja Rao, Attia Hosain, Khushwant Singh, Sudhin Ghose, G.V. Desani and Kamala Markandaya.

A few years ago, while I was sitting at my desk in Ivy Cottage (where I am sitting right now), a dapper little gentleman appeared in my doorway and introduced himself. He was none other than Mulk Raj Anand, aged ninety (he lived to be ninety-nine). He spent over an hour with me, talking about books, and I told him I'd read his novel *Coolie* while I was still at school in Simla—Simla being the setting for the novel. When he left, he thrust a ten-rupee note into little Siddharth's pocket. Siddharth, my great-grandson, was then only three or four and doesn't remember the occasion; but it was a nice gesture on the part of that Grand Old Man of Letters.

But I digress. I grow old and inclined to ramble. I should take T.S. Eliot's advice and wear the bottoms of my trousers rolled (and yes, they are beginning to look a little frayed and baggy). Is this what they call 'existential writing'? Or 'stream of consciousness'?

MY DESERT ISLAND

Back to my old school library. Yes, *my* library, since no one else seemed to bother with it. And from reading, it was only a short step to writing. A couple of spare exercise books were soon filled with my observations on school life—friends, foes, teachers, the headmaster's buxom wife, dormitory fights, the tuck shop and the mysterious disappearance of a senior prefect who was later found 'living in sin' with a fading film star (thirty years his senior) in a villa near Sanjauli. Well, that was his great escape from the tedium of boarding-school life.

It was not long before my magnum opus fell into the hands of my class teacher who passed it on to the headmaster, who sent for me and gave me a flogging. The exercise books were shredded and thrown into his wastepaper basket. End of my first literary venture.

But the seed had been sown, and I was not too upset. If the world outside could accommodate other writers, it could accommodate me too. My time would come.

In the meantime, there were books and authors to be discovered. A lifetime of reading lay ahead. Old books, new books, classics, thrillers, stories short and tall, travelogues, histories, biographies, comedies, comic strips, poems, memories, fantasies, fables...The adventure would end only when the lights went out for ever.

'Lights out!' called the master on duty, making his rounds of the dormitories.

Out went the lights.

And out came my little pocket torch, and whatever book I was immersed in, and with my head under the blanket I would read on for another twenty or thirty minutes, until sleep overcame me.

And in that sleep what dreams would come... dreams crowded with a wonderful cast of characters, all jumbled up, but each one distinct and alive, coming up to me and shaking me by the hand; Mr Pickwick, Sam Weller, Aunt Betsey Trotwood, Mr Dick, Tom Sawyer, Long John Silver, Lemuel Gulliver, the Mad Hatter, Alice, Mr Toad of Toad Hall, Hercule Poirot, Jeeves, Lord Emsworth, Kim, the Lama, Mowgli, Dick Tufpin, William Brown, Nero Wolfe, Ariel, Ali Baba, Snow White, Cinderella, Shakuntala, John Gilpin, Sherlock Holmes, Dr Watson, Peter and Wendy, Captain Hook, Richard Hannay, Allan Quatermain, Sexton Blake, Desperate Dan, old Uncle Tom Cobley and all.

Remember This Day

If you can get an entire year off from school when you are nine years old, and can have a memorable time with a great father, then that year has to be the best time of your life even if it is followed by sorrow and insecurity.

It was the result of my parents' separation at a time when my father was on active service in the RAF during World War II. He managed to keep me with him for a summer and winter, at various locations in New Delhi—Hailey Road, Atul Grove Lane, Scindia House—in apartments he had rented, as he was not permitted to keep a child in the quarters assigned to service personnel. This arrangement suited me perfectly, and I had a wonderful year in Delhi, going to the cinema, quaffing milkshakes, helping my father with his stamp collection; but this idyllic situation could not continue for ever, and when my father was transferred to Karachi he had no option but to put me in a boarding school.

This was the Bishop Cotton Preparatory School in Simla—or rather, Chhota Simla—where boys studied up to Class 4, after which they moved on to the senior school.

Although I was a shy boy, I had settled down quite well in the friendly atmosphere of this little school, but I did miss my fathers' companionship, and I was overjoyed when he came up to see me during the midsummer break. He had a couple of days' leave, and he could only take me out for a day, bringing me back to school in the evening.

I was so proud of him when he turned up in his dark blue R.A.F. uniform, a Flight Lieutenant's stripes very much in evidence as he had just been promoted. He was already forty, engaged in Codes and Ciphers and not flying much. He was short and stocky, getting bald, but smart in his uniforrn. I gave him a salute—I loved giving salutes—and he returned the salutation and followed it up with a hug and a kiss on my forehead.

'And what would you like to do today, son?' Let's go to Davico's,' I said. Davico's was the best restaurant in town, famous for its meringues, marzipans, curry-puffs and pastries. So to Davico's we went, where of course I gorged myself on confectionery as only a small schoolboy can do. 'Lunch is still a long way off, so let's take a walk,' suggested my father.

And provisioning ourselves with more pastries, we left the Mall and trudged up to the Monkey Temple at the top of Jakko Hill. Here we were relieved of the pastries by the monkeys, who simply snatched them away from my unwilling hands, and we came downhill in a hurry before I could get hungry again. Small boys and monkeys have much in common.

My father suggested a rickshaw ride around Elysium Hill, and this we did in style, swept along by four sturdy young rickshaw-pullers. My father took the opportunity of relating the story of Kipling's *Phantom Rickshaw* (this was before I discovered it in print), and a couple of other ghost stories designed to build up my appetite for lunch.

We ate at Wenger's (or was it Clark's?) and then—'Enough of ghosts, Ruskin. Let's go to the pictures.'

I loved going to the pictures. I know the Delhi cinemas intimately, and it hadn't taken me long to discover the Simla cinemas. There were three of them—

the Regal, the Ritz, and the Rivoli.

We went to the Rivoli. It was down near the ice-skating ring and the old Blessington Hotel. The film was about an ice-skater and starred Sonja Henie, a pretty young Norwegian Olympic champion who appeared in a number of Hollywood musicals. All she had to do was skate and look pretty, and this she did to perfection. I decided to fall in love with her. But by the time I grew up and finished school she'd stopped skating and making films! Whatever happened to Sonja Heme?

After the picture it was time to return to school. We walked all the way to Chhota Simla talking about what we'd do during the winter holidays, and where we would go when the War was over.

'I'll be in Calcutta now,' said my father. 'There are good bookshops there. And cinemas. And Chinese restaurants. And we'll buy more gramophone records, and add to the stamp collection.'

It was dusk when we walked slowly down the path to the school gate and playing-field. Two of my friends were waiting for me—Bimal and Riaz. My father spoke to them, asked about their homes. A bell started ringing. We said goodbye.

'Remember this day, Ruskin,' said my father.

He patted me gently on the head and walked away.

I never saw him again.

Three months later I heard that he had passed away in the military hospital in Calcutta.

I dream of him sometimes, and in my dream he is always the same, caring for me and leading me by the hand along old familiar roads.

And of course I remember that day. Over sixty-five years have passed, but it's as fresh as yesterday.

Letter to My Father

My Dear Dad,

Last week I decided to walk from the Dilaram Bazaar to Rajpur, a walk I hadn't undertaken for many years. It's only about five miles, along straight tree-lined road, houses most of the way, but here and there are open spaces where there are fields and patches of sal forest. The road hasn't changed much, but there is far more traffic than there used to be, which makes it noisy and dusty, detracting from the sylvan surroundings. All the same I enjoyed the walk—enjoyed the cool breeze that came down from the hills,—the rich variety of trees, the splashes of colour where bougainvillea trailed over porches and enjoyed the passing cyclists and bullock carts, for they were reminders of the old days when cars, trucks and buses were the exception rather than the rule.

A little way above the Dilaram Bazaar, just where the canal goes under the road, stands the old house we used to know as Melville Hall, where three generations of Melvilles had lived. It is now a government office and looks dirty and neglected. Beside it still stands the little cottage, or guest house, where you stayed for a few weeks while the separation from my mother was being made legal. Then I went to live with you in Delhi.

At the time you were a guest of the Melvilles, I was in boarding school, so I did not share the cottage with you, although I was to share a number of rooms, tents and RAf hutments with you during the next two or three years. But of course I knew the Melvilles; I would visit them during school holidays in the years after you died, and they always spoke affectionately of you. One of the sisters was particularly kind to me; I think it was she who gave you the use of the cottage. This was Mrs Chill—she'd lost her husband to cholera during their honeymoon, and never married again. But I always found her cheerful and good-natured, loading me with presents on birthdays and at Christmas. The kindest people are often those who have come through testing personal tragedies.

A young man on a bicycle stops beside me and asks if I remember him. 'Not with that terrible moustache,' I confess. 'Romi from Sisters Bazaar.' Yes, of course. And I do remember him, although it must be about ten years since we last met; he was just a schoolboy then. Now, he tells me, he's a teacher. Not very well paid, as he works in a small private school. But better than being unemployed, he says. I have to agree.

'You're a good teacher, I'm sure, Romi. And it's still a noble profession...'

He looks pleased as he cycles away. When I see boys on bicycles I am always taken back to my boyhood days in Debra. The roads in those uncrowded days were ideal for cyclists. Semi on his bicycle, riding down this very road in the light spring rain, provided me with the opening scene for my very first novel, *Room on the Roof*, written a couple of years after I'd said goodbye to Semi and Debra and even, for a time, India.

That's how I remember him best—on his bicycle, wearing shorts, turban slightly askew, always a song on his lips. He was just fifteen. I was a couple of years older, but wasn't much of a bicycle rider, always falling off the machine when I was supposed to dismount gracefully.

On one occasion I went sailing into a buffalo cart and fractured my forearm. Last year when Dr Murti, a senior citizen of the Doon, met me at a local function, he recalled how he had set my arm forty years ago. He was so nice to me that I forbore from telling him that my arm was still crooked.

Strictly an earth man, I have never really felt at ease with my feet off the ground. That's why I've been a walking person for most of my life. In planes, on ships, even in lifts, panic sets in.

As it did on that occasion when I was four or five, and you, Dad, decided to give me a treat by taking me on an Arab dhow across the Gulf of Kutch. Five minutes on that swinging, swaying sailing ship, was enough for me; I became so hysterical that I had to be taken off and rowed back to port. Not that the rowing boat was much better.

And then my mother thought I should go up with her in one those four-winged aeroplanes, a Tiger Moth I think—there's a photograph of it somewhere among my mementos—one of those contraptions that fell out of the sky without much assistance during the first World War. I think you could make them at home. Anyway, in this too I kicked and screamed with such abandon that the poor pilot had to be content with taxiing around the airfield and dropping me off at the first opportunity That same plane with the same pilot crashed a couple of months later, only reinforcing my fears about machines that could not stay anchored to the ground.

To return to Somi, he was one of those friends I never saw again as an adult, so he remains transfixed in my memory as eternal youth, bright and forever loving… Meeting boyhood friends again after long intervals can often be disappointing, even disconcerting. Mere survival leaves its mark. Success is even more disfiguring. Those who climb to the top of a profession, or who seek the pinnacles of power, usually have to pay a heavy price for it, both physically and spiritually. It sounds like a cliche but it's true that money can't buy good health or a serene state of mind—especially the latter. You can fly to the ends of the earth in search of the best climate or the best medical treatment and the chances are that you will have to keep flying! Poverty is not ennobling—far from it—but it does at least teach you to make the most out of every rule.

I have often dreamt of Somi, and it is always the same dream, year after year, for over forty years. We meet in a fairground, set up on Debra's old parade-ground which has seen better days. In the dream I am a man but he is still a boy. We wander through the fairground, enjoying all that it has to offer, and when the dream ends we are still in that fairground which probably represents heaven.

Heaven. Is that the real heaven—the perfect place with the perfect companion? And if you and I meet again, Dad, will you look the same, and will I be a small boy or an old man?

In my dreams of you I meet you on a busy street, after many lost years, and you receive me with the same old warmth, but where were you all those missing years? A traveller in another dimension, perhaps, returning occasionally just to see if I am all right.

Ruskin Bond

Our Great Escape

It had been a lonely winter for a fourteen-year-old. I had spent the first few weeks of the vacation with my mother and stepfather in Dehra. Then they left for Delhi, and I was pretty much on my own. Of course, the servants were there to take care of my needs, but there was no one to keep me company. I would wander off in the mornings, taking some path up the hills, come back home for lunch, read a bit and then stroll off again till it was time for dinner. Sometimes I walked up to my grandparents' house, but it seemed so different now, with people I didn't know occupying the house.

The three-month winter break over, I was almost eager to return to my boarding school in Shimla.

It wasn't as though I had many friends at school. I needed a friend but it was not easy to find one among a horde of rowdy, pea-shooting eighth formers, who carved their names on desks and stuck chewing gum on the class teacher's chair. Had I grown up with other children, I might have developed a taste for schoolboy anarchy; but in sharing my father's loneliness after his separation from my mother, and in being bereft of any close family ties, I had turned into a premature adult.

After a month in the eighth form, I began to notice a new boy, Omar, and then only because he was a quiet, almost taciturn person who took no part in the form's feverish attempt to imitate the Marx Brothers at the circus. He showed no resentment at the prevailing anarchy, nor did he make a move to participate in it. Once he caught me looking at him, and he smiled ruefully, tolerantly. Did I sense another adult in the class? Someone who was a little older than his years?

Even before we began talking to each other, Omar and I developed an understanding of sorts, and we'd nod almost respectfully to each other when we met in the classroom corridors or the environs of the dining hall or the dormitory. We were not in the same house. The house system practised its own form of apartheid, whereby a member of one house was not expected to fraternize with someone belonging to another. Those public schools certainly knew how to clamp you into compartments. However, these barriers vanished when Omar and I found ourselves selected for the School Colts' hockey team; Omar as a full-back, I as the goalkeeper.

The taciturn Omar now spoke to me occasionally, and we combined well on the field of play. A good understanding is needed between a goalkeeper and a full-back. We were on the same wavelength. I anticipated his moves, he was familiar with mine. Years later, when I read Conrad's *The Secret Sharer*, I thought of Omar.

It wasn't until we were away from the confines of school, classroom and dining hall that our friendship flourished. The hockey team travelled to Sanawar on the next mountain range, where we were to play a couple of matches against our old rivals, the Lawrence Royal Military School. This had been my father's old school, so I was keen to explore its grounds and peep into its classrooms.

Omar and I were thrown together a good deal during the visit to Sanawar, and in our more leisurely moments, strolling undisturbed around a school where we were guests and not pupils, we exchanged life histories and other confidences. Omar, too, had lost his father—had I sensed that before?—shot in some tribal encounter on the Frontier, for he hailed from the lawless lands beyond Peshawar. A wealthy uncle was seeing to Omar's education.

We wandered into the school chapel, and there I found my father's name—A.A. Bond—on the school's roll of honour board: old boys who had lost their lives while serving during the two World Wars.

'What did his initials stand for?' asked Omar.

'Aubrey Alexander.'

'Unusual name, like yours. Why did your parents call you Rusty?'

'I am not sure.' I told him about the book I was writing. It was my first one and was called *Nine Months* (the length of the school term, not a pregnancy), and it described some of the happenings at school and lampooned a few of our teachers. I had filled three slim exercise books with this premature literary project, and I allowed Omar to go through them. He must have been my first reader and critic.

'They're very interesting,' he said, 'but you'll get into trouble if someone finds them, especially Mr Fisher.'

I have to admit it wasn't great literature. I was better at hockey and football. I made some spectacular saves, and we won our matches against Sanawar. When we returned to Shimla, we were school heroes for a couple of days and lost some of our reticence; we were even a little more forthcoming with other boys. And then Mr Fisher, my housemaster, discovered my literary opus, *Nine Months*, under my mattress, and took it away and read it (as he told me later) from cover to cover. Corporal punishment then being in vogue, I was given six of the best with a springy Malacca cane, and my manuscript was torn up and deposited in Mr Fisher's wastepaper basket. All I had to show for my efforts were some purple welts on my bottom. These were proudly displayed to all who were interested, and I was a hero for another two days.

'Will you go away too when the British leave India?' Omar asked me one day.

'I don't think so,' I said. 'I don't have anyone to go back to in England, and my guardian, Mr Harrison, too seems to have no intention of going back.'

'Everyone is saying that our leaders and the British are going to divide the country. Shimla will be in India, Peshawar in Pakistan!'

'Oh, it won't happen,' I said glibly. 'How can they cut up such a big country?' But even as we chatted about the possibility, Nehru, Jinnah and Mountbatten, and all

OUR GREAT ESCAPE

those who mattered, were preparing their instruments for major surgery.

Before their decision impinged on our lives and everyone else's, we found a little freedom of our own, in an underground tunnel that we discovered below the third flat.

It was really part of an old, disused drainage system, and when Omar and I began exploring it, we had no idea just how far it extended. After crawling along on our bellies for some twenty feet, we found ourselves in complete darkness. Omar had brought along a small pencil torch, and with its help we continued writhing forward (moving backwards would have been quite impossible) until we saw a glimmer of light at the end of the tunnel. Dusty, musty, very scruffy, we emerged at last on to a grassy knoll, a little way outside the school boundary.

It's always a great thrill to escape beyond the boundaries that adults have devised. Here we were in unknown territory. To travel without passports—that would be the ultimate in freedom!

But more passports were on their way—and more boundaries.

Lord Mountbatten, viceroy and governor-general-to-be, came for our Founder's Day and gave away the prizes. I had won a prize for something or the other, and mounted the rostrum to receive my book from this towering, handsome man in his pinstripe suit. Bishop Cotton's was then the premier school of India, often referred to as the 'Eton of the East'. Viceroys and governors had graced its functions. Many of its boys had gone on to eminence in the civil services and armed forces. There was one 'old boy' about whom they maintained a stolid silence—General Dyer, who had ordered the massacre at Amritsar and destroyed the trust that had been building up between Britain and India.

Now Mountbatten spoke of the momentous events that were happening all around us—the War had just come to an end, the United Nations held out the promise of a world living in peace and harmony, and India, an equal partner with Britain, would be among the great nations...

A few weeks later, Bengal and the Punjab provinces were bisected. Riots flared up across northern India, and there was a great exodus of people crossing the newly-drawn frontiers of Pakistan and India. Homes were destroyed, thousands lost their lives.

OUR GREAT ESCAPE

The common room radio and the occasional newspaper kept us abreast of events, but in our tunnel, Omar and I felt immune from all that was happening, worlds away from all the pillage, murder and revenge. And outside the tunnel, on the pine knoll below the school, there was fresh untrodden grass, sprinkled with clover and daisies; the only sounds we heard were the hammering of a woodpecker and the distant insistent call of the Himalayan Barbet. Who could touch us there?

'And when all the wars are done,' I said, 'a butterfly will still be beautiful.'

'Did you read that somewhere?'

'No, it just came into my head.'

'Already you're a writer.'

'No, I want to play hockey for India or football for Arsenal. Only winning teams!'

'You can't win forever. Better to be a writer.'

When the monsoon arrived, the tunnel was flooded, the drain choked with rubble. We were allowed out to the cinema to see Laurence Olivier's *Hamlet*, a film that did nothing to raise our spirits on a wet and gloomy afternoon; but it was our last picture that year, because communal riots suddenly broke out in Shimla's Lower

Bazaar, an area that was still much as Kipling had described it—'a man who knows his way there can defy all the police of India's summer capital'—and we were confined to school indefinitely.

One morning after prayers in the chapel, the headmaster announced that the Muslim boys—those who had their homes in what was now Pakistan—would have to be evacuated, sent to their homes across the border with an armed convoy.

The tunnel no longer provided an escape for us. The bazaar was out of bounds. The flooded playing field was deserted. Omar and I sat on a damp wooden bench and talked about the future in vaguely hopeful terms, but we didn't solve any problems. Mountbatten and Nehru and Jinnah were doing all the solving.

It was soon time for Omar to leave—he left along with some fifty other boys from Lahore, Pindi and Peshawar. The rest of us—Hindus, Christians, Parsis—helped them load their luggage into the waiting trucks. A couple of boys broke down and wept. So did our departing school captain, a Pathan who had been known for his stoic and unemotional demeanour. Omar waved cheerfully to me and I waved back. We had vowed to meet again some day.

OUR GREAT ESCAPE

The convoy got through safely enough. There was only one casualty—the school cook, who had strayed into an off-limits area in the foothill town of Kalika and been set upon by a mob. He wasn't seen again.

Towards the end of the school year, just as we were all getting ready to leave for the school holidays, I received a letter from Omar. He told me something about his new school and how he missed my company and our games and our tunnel to freedom. I replied and gave him my home address, but I did not hear from him again.

Some seventeen or eighteen years later, I did get news of Omar, but in an entirely different context. India and Pakistan were at war, and in a bombing raid over Ambala, not far from Shimla, a Pakistani plane was shot down. Its crew died in the crash. One of them, I learnt later, was Omar.

Did he, I wonder, get a glimpse of the playing fields we knew so well as boys? Perhaps memories of his schooldays flooded back as he flew over the foothills. Perhaps he remembered the tunnel through which we were able to make our little escape to freedom.

But there are no tunnels in the sky.

Reading Was My Religion

The RAF had undertaken to pay for my schooling, so I was able to continue at the Bishop Cotton School. Back in Shimla I found a sympathetic soul in Mr Jones, an ex-army Welshman who taught us divinity. He did not have the qualifications to teach us anything else, but I think I learnt more from him than from most of our more qualified staff. He had even got me to read the Bible (King James version) for the classical simplicity of its style.

Mr Jones got on well with small boys, one reason being that he never punished them. Alone among the philistines, he was the only teacher to stand out against corporal punishment. He waged a lone campaign against the custom of caning boys for their misdemeanours, and in this respect was thought to be a little eccentric, and he lost his seniority because of his refusal to administer physical punishment.

But there was nothing eccentric about Mr Jones, unless it was the pet pigeon that followed him everywhere and sometimes perched on his bald head. He managed to keep the pigeon (and his cigar) out of the classroom, but his crowded, untidy bachelor quarters reeked of cigar smoke.

He had a passion for the works of Dickens, and when he discovered that I had read *Nicholas Nickleby* and *Sketches by Box*, he allowed me to look at his set of the *Complete Works*, with the illustrations by Phiz. I launched into *David Copperfield*, which I thoroughly enjoyed, identifying myself with young David, his triumphs and tribulations. After reading *Copperfield* I decided it was a fine thing to be a writer. The seed had already been sown, and although in my imagination I still saw myself as an Arsenal goalkeeper or a Gene Kelly-type tap dancer, I think I knew in my heart that I was best suited to the written word. I was topping the class in essay writing; although I had an aversion to studying the texts that were prescribed for English Literature classes.

Mr Jones, with his socialist, Dickensian viewpoint,

had an aversion to P.G. Wodehouse, whose comic novels I greatly enjoyed. He told me that these novels glamorized the most decadent aspects of upper-class; English life (which was probably true), and that only recently, during the war (when he was interned in France), Wodehouse had been making propaganda broadcasts on behalf of Germany. This was true, too; although years later when I read the texts of those broadcasts (in *Performing Fled*), they seemed harmless enough.

But Mr Jones did have a point. Wodehouse was hopelessly out of date, for when I went to England after leaving school, I couldn't find anyone remotely resembling a Wodehouse character—except perhaps Ukridge, who was always borrowing money from his friends in order to set up some business or the other. He was universal.

The school library, the Anderson Library, was fairly well-stocked, and it was to be something of a haven for me over the next three years. There were always writers, past or present, to 'discover'—and I still have a tendency to ferret out writers who have been ignored, neglected or forgotten.

After *Copperfield*, the novel that most influenced

me was Hugh Walpole's *Fortitude*, an epic account of another young writer in the making. Its opening line still acts as a clarion call when I feel depressed or as though I am getting nowhere: 'Tisn't life that matters! Tis the courage you bring to it.'

Walpole's more ambitious works have been forgotten, but his stories and novels of the macabre are still worth reading—'Mr Perrin and Mr Traill', 'Portrait of a Man with Red Hair', 'The White Tower' and, of course, *Fortitude*. I returned to it last year and found it was still stirring stuff.

But life wasn't all books. At the age of fifteen I was at my best as a football goalkeeper, hockey player and athlete. I was also acting in school plays and taking part in debates. I wasn't much of a boxer—the sport I disliked—but I had learnt to use my head to good effect, and managed to get myself disqualified by butting the other fellow in the head or midriff. As all games were compulsory, I had to overcome my fear of water and learn to swim a little. Mr Jones taught me to do the breast stroke, saying it was more suited to my temperament than the splash and dash stuff.

The only thing I couldn't do was sing, and although I loved listening to great singers, from Caruso to Gigli,

I couldn't sing a note. Our music teacher, Mrs Knight, put me in the school choir because, she said, I looked like a choir boy, all pink and shining in a cassock and surplice, but she forbade me from actually singing. I was to open my mouth with the others, but on no account was I to allow any sound to issue from it.

This took me back to the convent in Mussoorie where I had been given piano lessons, probably at my father's behest. The nun who was teaching me would get so exasperated with my stubborn inability to strike the right chord or play the right notes that she would crack me over the knuckles with a ruler, thus effectively putting to an end any interest I might have had in learning to play a musical instrument. Mr Priestley's violin in prep-school, and now Mrs Knight's organ-playing were none too inspiring.

Insensitive though I may have been to high notes and low notes, *diminuendos and crescendos*, I was nevertheless sensitive to sound, such as birdsong, the hum of the breeze playing in tall trees, the rustle of autumn leaves, crickets chirping, water splashing and murmuring brooks, the sea sighing on the sand—all natural sounds, that indicated a certain harmony in the natural world.

READING WAS MY RELIGION

Man-made sounds—the roar planes, the blare of horns, the thunder of trucks and engines, the baying of a crowd—are usually ugly, but some gifted humans have risen to create great music. We must not then scorn the also-rans, who come down hard on their organ pedals or emulate cicadas with their violin playing.

Although I was quite popular at BCS, after Omar's departure I did not have many close friends. There was, of course, young A, my junior by two years, who followed me everywhere until I gave in and took him to the pictures in town, or fed him at the tuck shop.

There were just one or two boys who actually read books for pleasure. We tend to think of that era as one when there were no distractions such as television, computer games and the like. But reading has always been a minority pastime. People say children don't read any more. This may be true of the vast majority, but I know many boys and girls who enjoy reading—far more than I encountered when I was a schoolboy. In those days there were comics and the radio and the cinema. I went to the cinema whenever I could, but that did not keep me from reading almost everything that came my way. And so it is today. Book readers are special people, and they will always turn to books as the ultimate pleasure. Those who do not read are the unfortunate ones. There's nothing wrong with them, but they are missing out on one of life's compensations and rewards. A great book is a friend that never lets you down. You can return to it again and again, and the joy first derived from it will still be there.

I think it is fair to say that, when I was a boy, reading was my true religion. It helped me discover my soul.

School Days, Rule Days

Here Comes Mr Oliver

Apart from being our Scoutmaster, Mr Oliver taught us maths, a subject in which I had some difficulty obtaining pass marks. Sometimes I scraped through; usually I got something like twenty or thirty out of a hundred. 'Failed again, Bond,' Mr Oliver would say. 'What will you do when you grow up?' 'Become a scoutmaster, sir.'

'Scoutmasters don't get paid. It's an honorary job. You could become a cook. That would suit you.' He hadn't forgotten our Scout camp, when I had been the camp's cook.

If Mr Oliver was in a good mood, he'd give me grace marks, passing me by a mark or two. He wasn't a hard man, but he seldom smiled. He was very dark, thin, stooped (from a distance he looked like a question mark), and balding. He was about forty, still a bachelor, and it was said that he had been unlucky in love—that the girl he was going to marry jilted him at the last moment, running away with a sailor while Mr Oliver waited at the church, ready for the wedding ceremony. No wonder he always had such a sorrowful look.

Mr Oliver did have one inseparable companion: a dachshund, a snappy little 'sausage' of a dog, who looked upon the human race, and especially small boys, with a certain disdain and frequent hostility. We called him Hitler. (This was 1945, and the dictator was at the end of his tether.) He was impervious to overtures of friendship, and if you tried to pat or stroke him he would do his best to bite your fingers or your shin or ankle. However, he was devoted to Mr Oliver and followed him everywhere except into the classroom; this our Headmaster would not allow. You remember that old nursery rhyme:

> *Mary had a little lamb,*
> *Its fleece was white as snow,*
> *And everywhere that Mary went*
> *The lamb was sure to go.*

Well, we made up our own version of the rhyme, and I

HERE COMES MR OLIVER

must confess to having had a hand in its composition. It went like this:

> *Olly had a little dog,*
> *It was never out of sight,*
> *And everyone that Olly met*
> *The dog was sure to bite!*

It followed him about the school grounds. It followed him when he took a walk through the pines to the Brockhuist tennis courts. It followed him into town and home again. Mr Oliver had no other friend, no other companion. The dog slept at the foot of Mr Oliver's bed. It did not sit at the breakfast table, but it had buttered toast for breakfast and soup and crackers for dinner. Mr Oliver had to take his lunch in the dining hall with the staff and boys, but he had an arrangement with one of the bearers whereby a plate of dal, rice and chapattis made its way to Mr Oliver's quarters and his well-fed pet.

And then tragedy struck.

Mr Oliver and Hitler were returning to school after an evening walk through the pines. It was dusk, and the light was fading fast. Out of the shadows of the trees emerged a lean and hungry panther. It pounced on the hapless dog, flung it across the road, seized it between its powerful jaws, and made off with its victim into the darkness of the forest.

Mr Oliver was untouched but frozen into immobility for at least a minute. Then he began calling for help. Some bystanders, who had witnessed the incident, began shouting too. Mr Oliver ran into the forest, but there was no sign of dog or panther.

Mr Oliver appeared to be a broken man. He went about his duties with a poker face, but we could all tell that he was grieving for his lost companion, for in the classroom he was listless and indifferent to whether or not we followed his calculations on the blackboard. In times of personal loss, the Highest Common Factor made no sense.

Mr Oliver was no longer seen going on his evening walk. He stayed in his room, playing cards with himself. He played with his food, pushing most of it aside. There were no chapattis to send home.

'Olly needs another pet,' said Bimal, wise in the ways of adults.

'Or a wife,' said Tata, who thought on those lines.

'He's too old. He must be over forty.'

'A pet is best,' I said. 'What about a parrot?'

HERE COMES MR OLIVER

'You can't take a parrot for a walk,' said Bimal. 'Oily wants someone to walk beside him.'

'A cat maybe.'

'Hitler hated cats. A cat would be an insult to Hitler's memory.'

'Then he needs another dachshund. But there aren't any around here.'

'Any dog will do. We'll ask Chimpu to get us a pup.'

Chimpu ran the tuck shop. He lived in the Chotta Shimla bazaar, and occasionally we would ask him to bring us tops or marbles, a corflic or other little things that we couldn't get in school. Five of us Boy Scouts contributed a rupee each, which we gave to Chimpu and asked him to get us a pup. 'A good breed,' we told him, 'not a mongrel.'

The next evening Chimpu turned up with a pup that seemed to be a combination of at least five different breeds, all good ones no doubt. One ear lay flat, the other stood upright. It was spotted like a Dalmatian, but it had the legs of a spaniel and the tail of a Pomeranian. It was floppy and playful, and the tail wagged a lot, which was more than Hitler's ever did.

'It's quite pretty,' said Tata. 'Must be a female.'

'He may not want a female,' said Bimal.

'Let's give it a try,' I said.

'During our play hour, before the bell rang for supper, we left the pup on the steps outside Mr Oliver's front door. Then we knocked, and sped into the hibiscus bush that lined the pathway.

Mr Oliver opened the door. He locked down at the pup with an expressionless face. The pup began to paw at Mr Oliver's shoes, loosening one of his laces in the process.

'Away with you!' muttered Mr Oliver. 'Buzz off!' And he pushed the pup away, gently but firmly, and closed the door.

We went through the same procedure again, but the result was much the same. We now had a playful pup on our hands, and Chimpu had gone home for the night. We would have to conceal it in the dormitory.

At first we hid it in Bimal's locker, but it began to yelp and struggled to get out. Tata took it into the shower room, but it wouldn't stay there either. It began running around the dormitory, playing with socks, shoes, slippers, and anything else it could get hold of.

'Watch out!' hissed one of the boys. 'Here comes Fisher!'

Mrs Fisher, the Headmaster's wife, was on her

HERE COMES MR OLIVER

nightly rounds, checking to make sure we were all in bed and not up to some natural mischief. I grabbed the pup and hid it under my blanket. It was quiet there, happy to nibble at my toes. When Mrs Fisher had gone, I let the pup loose again, and for the rest of the night it had the freedom of the dormitory.

At the crack of dawn, before first light, Bimal and I sped out of the dormitory in our pyjamas, taking the pup with us. We banged hard on Mr Oliver's door, and kept knocking until we heard footsteps approaching. As soon as the door was slowly opened, we pushed the pup inside and ran for our lives.

Mr Oliver came to class as usual, but there was no pup with him. Three or four days passed, and still no sign of the pup! Had he passed it on to someone else, or simply let it wander off on its own?

'Here comes Oily!' called Bimal, from our vantage point near the school bell.

Mr Oliver was setting out for his evening walk. He was carrying a strong walnut-wood walking stick—to keep panthers at bay, no doubt. He looked neither left nor right, and if he noticed us watching him, Mr Oliver gave no sign. But then, scurrying behind him was the pup! The creature of many good breeds was accompanying Mr Oliver on his walk. It had been well brushed and was wearing a bright red collar. Like Mr Oliver, it took no notice of us. It walked along beside its new master.

Mr Oliver and the little pup were soon inseparable companions, and my friends and I were quite pleased with ourselves. Mr Oliver gave absolutely no indication that he knew where the pup had come from, but when the end-of-term exams were over, and Bimal and I were sure that we had failed our maths papers, we were surprised to find that we had passed after all—with grace marks!

'Good old Oily!' said Bimal. 'So he knew all the time.' Tata, of course, did not need grace marks—he was a wizard at maths—but Bimal and I decided we would thank Mr Oliver for his kindness.

'Nothing to thank me for,' said Mr Oliver gruffly, but with a twist at the corners of his mouth, which was the nearest he came to a smile. 'I've seen enough of you two in junior school. It's high time you went up to the senior school—and God help you there!'

The Lady in White

(An extract from Mr Oliver's diary)

A ghost on the main highway past our school. She's known as Bhoot-Aunty—a spectral apparition who appears to motorists on their way to Sanjauli. She waves down passing cars and asks for a lift; and if you give her one, you are liable to have an accident.

This lady in white is said to be the revenant of a young woman who was killed in a car accident not far from here, a few months ago. Several motorists claim to have seen her. Oddly enough, pedestrians don't come across her.

Miss Ramola, Miss D'Costa and I are the exceptions.

I had accompanied some of the staff and boys to the girls' school to see a hockey match, and afterwards the ladies asked me to accompany them back as it was getting dark and they had heard there was a panther about.

'The only panther is Mr Oliver,' remarked Miss D'Costa, who was spending the weekend with Anjali Ramola.

'Such a harmless panther,' said Anjali.

I wanted to say that panthers always attack women who wore outsize earrings (such as Miss D'Costa's) but my gentlemanly upbringing prevented a rude response.

As we turned the corner near our school gate, Miss D'Costa cried out, 'Oh, do you see that strange woman sitting on the parapet wall?'

Sure enough, a figure clothed in white was resting against the wall, its face turned away from us.

'Could it—could it be—Bhoot-Aunty?' stammered Miss D'Costa.

The two ladies stood petrified in the middle of the road. I stepped forward and asked, 'Who are you, and what can we do for you?'

The ghostly apparition raised its arms, got up suddenly and rushed past me. Miss D'Costa let out a shriek. Anjali turned and fled. The figure in white flapped about, then tripped over its own winding-cloth, and fell in front of me.

THE LADY IN WHITE

As it got to its feet, the white sheet fell away and revealed—Mirchi!

'You wicked boy!' I shouted. 'Just what do you think you are up to?'

'Sorry, sir,' he gasped. 'It's just a joke. Bhoot-Aunty, sir!' And he fled the scene.

When the ladies had recovered, I saw them home and promised to deal severely with Mirchi. But on second thoughts I decided to overlook his prank. Miss D'Costa deserved getting a bit of a fright for calling me a panther.

I had picked up Mirchi's bedsheet from the road, and after supper I carried it into the dormitory and placed it on his bed without any comment. He was about to get into bed, and looked up at me in some apprehension.

'Er—thank you, sir,' he said.

'An enjoyable performance,' I told him. 'Next time, make it more convincing.'

After making sure that all the dormitory and corridor lights were out, I went for a quiet walk on my own. I am not averse to a little solitude. I have no objection to my own company. This is different from loneliness, which can assail you even when you are amongst people.

Being a misfit in a group of boisterous party-goers can be a lonely experience. But being alone as a matter of choice is one of life's pleasures.

As I passed the same spot where Mirchi had got up to mischief, I was surprised to see a woman sitting by herself on the low parapet wall. *Another lover of solitude*, I thought. I gave her no more than a glance. She was looking the other way. A pale woman, dressed very simply. I had gone some distance when a thought suddenly came to me. Had I just passed Bhoot-Aunty? The real bhoot? The pale woman in white had seemed rather ethereal.

I stopped, turned, and looked again.

The lady had vanished.

Missing Person: H.M.

(An extract from Mr Oliver's diary)

Sensational disappearance of Headmaster.
He hasn't been seen for two days, three nights. Stepped out of his house just after daybreak, saying he was going for a walk, and did not return.

Was he taken by the leopard? Had he been kidnapped?

Had he lost his footing and fallen off a cliff?

H.M.'s wife in distress. Police called in. Inspector Keemat Lal, C.I.D. asks questions of everyone but is none the wiser, it appears. He is more at home with dead bodies than missing persons.

Finally he asks: 'Did he take anything with him? A bag, a suitcase? Did he have money on him?'

'I don't know about money,' said Mrs H. 'But he took his gun.'

'He must have gone after that leopard,' I surmised. 'I hope the leopard hasn't got him.'

And so once again we all trooped off into the forest—the Inspector, two constables, Mr Tuli, four senior boys (including Tata and Mirchi) and myself. After two hours of slogging through mist and drizzle we made enquiries in two neighbouring villages without receiving much by way of information or encouragement. One small boy told us he had seen a man with a gun wandering about further down the valley, so we trudged on for another two hours, the portly Inspector Keemat Lal perspiring profusely and cursing all the while. Some of our police officers acquire a colourful vocabulary in the course of their careers.

Trudging back to school, I got into conversation with Inspector Keemat Lal, who had a tendency to reminisce. 'What was the closest shave you ever had?' I asked. 'The closest shave. Oddly enough, it was when I went into a barber's shop for a shave. This was in Agra, when I was a sub-inspector.'

'What happened?'

'Well, the barber was a friendly enough fellow, a bit

MISSING PERSON: H.M.

of a joker. After lathering my cheeks and stropping his razor, he casually remarked, 'How easy it would be for me to cut your throat, sir!'

'I didn't take him seriously, but I resented his familiarity and the bad taste of his remark. So I got up from the chair, wiped the soap from my face, and walked out of the shop. The next customer gratefully took my place.'

'Of course he was joking,' I said.

'So I thought. But next day, when I went on duty, I learnt that he had cut the throat of one of his customers. Quite possibly the one who took my place. The barber was a homicidal maniac. He had been acting strangely for some time, and something had snapped in his head.'

'Getting up and leaving—that was good reasoning on your part.'

'No, reasoning didn't come into it. It was pure instinct. When it comes to self-preservation, instinct is more reliable than reason.'

No sign of H.M., no further news of his whereabouts, not even a sighting. The return journey was even more arduous as it was uphill all the way. Everyone complained of thirst, and at the first small shop we came to, I had to buy soft drinks for everyone, although the policemen were hoping for something stronger. Arriving at school, we straggled into H.M.'s garden just as it was getting dark. Mrs H opened the front door for us. She was beaming. And no wonder. For there was H.M. sitting in his favourite armchair, enjoying a cup of tea!

No thanks for our efforts and no tea either, not even for the policemen.

It transpired that H.M. had been feeling very depressed for some time, on account of his being unable to master the intricacies of Kreisler's Violin Sonata, and in a fit of frustration and anger he had smashed his violin, then taken off with his gun, meaning to shoot himself. He had spent a day in the forest, a night in a seedy hotel, and a day and a night in the Barog tunnel and railway waiting room, before deciding that the Violin Sonata could wait for another violin.

'Cracked,' said Mirchi, not for the first time. 'Sir, are all Headmasters like this?'

'No, of course not,' I hastened to assure him. 'Some of them are quite sane.'

Miss Babcock's Big Toe

If two people are thrown together for a long time, they can became either close friends or sworn enemies. Thus, it was with Tata and me when we both went down with mumps and had to spend a fortnight together in the school hospital. It wasn't really a hospital—just a five-bed ward in a small cottage on the approach road to our prep-school in Chhota Shimla. It was supervised by a retired nurse, an elderly matron called Miss Babcock, who was all but stone deaf.

Miss Babcock was an able nurse, but she was a fidgety, fussy person, always dashing about from ward to dispensary and to her own room, as a result the boys called her Miss Shuttlecock. As she couldn't hear us, she didn't mind. But her hearing difficulty did create something of a problem, both for her and for her patients. If someone in the ward felt ill late at night, he had to shout or ring a bell, and she heard neither. So, someone had to get up and fetch her.

Miss Babcock devised an ingenious method of waking her in an emergency. She tied a long piece of string to the foot of the sick person's bed; then took the other end of the string to her own room, where, upon retiring for the night, she tied it to her big toe.

A vigorous pull on the string from the sick person, and Miss Babcock would be wide awake!

Now, what could be more tempting to a small boy than—such a device? The string was tied to the foot of Tata's bed, and he was a restless fellow, always wanting water, always complaining of aches and pains. And sometimes, out of plain mischief, he would give several tugs on that string until Miss Babcock arrived with a pill or a glass of water.

'You'll have my toe off by morning,' she complained. 'You don't have to pull quite so hard.'

And what was worse, when Tata did fall asleep, he snored to high heaven and nothing could wake him! I had to lie awake most of the night, listening to his rhythmic snoring. It was like a trumpet tuning up or a bullfrog calling to its mates.

MISS BABCOCK'S BIG TOE

Fortunately, a couple of nights later, we were joined in the ward by Bimal, a friend and fellow 'feather', who had also contracted mumps. One night of Tata's snoring, and Bimal resolved to do something about it.

'Wait until he's fast asleep,' said Bimal, 'and then we'll carry his bed outside and leave him in the veranda.' We did more than that. As Tata commenced his nightly imitation of all the wind instruments in the London Philharmonic Orchestra, we lifted up his bed as gently as possible and carried it out into the garden, putting it down beneath the nearest pine tree.

'It's healthier outside,' said Bimal, justifying our action. 'All this fresh air should cure him.' Leaving Tata to serenade the stars, we returned to the ward expecting to enjoy a good night's sleep. So did Miss Babcock.

However, we couldn't sleep long. We were woken by Miss Babcock running around the ward screaming, 'Where's Tata? Where's Tata?' She ran outside, and we followed dutifully, barefoot, in our pyjamas.

The bed stood where we had put it down, but of Tata, there was no sign. Instead, there was a large black-faced langur at the foot of the bed, baring its teeth in a grin of disfavour.

'Tata's gone,' gasped Miss Babcock.

'He must be a sleepwalker.' said Bimal.

'Maybe the leopard took him,' I said. Just then there was a commotion in the shrubbery at the end of the garden and shouting, 'Help, help!' Tata emerged from the bushes, followed by several lithe, long-tailed langurs, merrily giving chase. Apparently, he'd woken up at the crack of dawn to find his bed surrounded by a gang of inquisitive simians. They had meant no harm, but Tata had panicked, and made a dash for life and liberty, running into the forest instead of into the cottage. We got Tata and his bed back into the ward, and Miss Babcock took his temperature and gave him a dose of salts. Oddly enough, in all the excitement no one asked how Tata and his bed had travelled in the night.

And strangely, he did not snore the following night; so perhaps the pine-scented night air really helped. Needless to say, we all soon recovered from the mumps, and Miss Babcock's big toe received a well-deserved rest.

A Dreadful Gurgle

Have you ever woken up in the night to find someone in your bed who wasn't supposed to be there? Well, it happened to me when I was at boarding school in Shimla, many years ago.

I was sleeping in the senior dormitory, along with some twenty other boys, and my bed was positioned in a corner of the long room, at some distance from the others. There was no shortage of pranksters in our dormitory, and one had to look out for the introduction of stinging-nettle or pebbles or possibly even a small lizard under the bedsheets. But I wasn't prepared for a body in my bed.

At first I thought a sleep-walker had mistakenly got into my bed, and I tried to push him out, muttering, 'Devinder, get back into your own bed. There isn't room for two of us.' Devinder was a notorious sleep-walker, who had even ended up on the roof on one occasion.

But it wasn't Devinder.

Devinder was a short boy, and this fellow was a tall, lanky person. His feet stuck out of the blanket at the foot of the bed. *It must be Ranjit*, I thought. Ranjit had huge feet.

'Ranjit,' I hissed. 'Stop playing the fool, and get back to your own bed.'

No response.

I tried pushing, but without success. The body was heavy and inert. It was also very cold.

I lay there wondering who it could be, and then it began to dawn on me that the person beside me wasn't breathing, and the horrible realization came to me that there was a corpse in my bed. How did it get there, and what was I to do about it?

'Vishal,' I called out to a boy who was sleeping a short distance away. 'Vishal, wake up, there's a corpse in the bed!'

Vishal did wake up. 'You're dreaming, Bond. Go to sleep and stop disturbing everyone.'

Just then there was a groan followed by a dreadful gurgle, from the body beside me. I shot out of the bed,

A DREADFUL GURGLE

shouting at the top of my voice, waking up the entire dormitory.

Lights came on. There was total confusion. The Housemaster came running. I told him and everyone else what had happened. They came to my bed and had a good look at it. But there was no one there.

On my insistence, I was moved to the other end of the dormitory. The house prefect, Johnson, took over my former bed. Two nights passed without further excitement, and a couple of boys started calling me a funk and a scaredy-cat. My response was to punch one of them on the nose.

Then, on the third night, we were all woken by several ear-splitting shrieks, and Johnson came charging across the dormitory, screaming that two icy hands had taken him by the throat and tried to squeeze the life out of him. Lights came on, and the poor old Housemaster came dashing in again. We calmed Johnson down and put him in a spare bed. The Housemaster shone his torch on the boy's face and neck, and sure enough, we saw several bruises on his flesh and the outline of a large hand.

Next day, the offending bed was removed from the dormitory, but it was a few days before Johnson recovered from the shock. He was kept in the infirmary until the bruises disappeared. But for the rest of the year he was a nervous wreck.

Our nursing sister, who had looked after the infirmary for many years, recalled that some twenty years earlier, a boy called Tomkins had died suddenly in the dormitory. He was very tall for his age, but apparently suffered from a heart problem. That day he had taken part in a football match, and had gone to bed looking pale and exhausted. Early next morning, when the bell rang for morning gym, he was found stiff and cold, having died during the night.

'He died peacefully, poor boy,' recalled our nursing sister.

But I'm not so sure. I can still hear that dreadful gurgle from the body in my bed. And there was the struggle with Johnson. No, there was nothing peaceful about that death. Tomkins had gone most unwillingly...

A Face in the Dark

It may give you some idea of rural humour if I begin this tale with an anecdote that concerns me. I was walking alone through a village at night when I met an old man carrying a lantern. I found, to my surprise, that the man was blind. 'Old man,' I asked, 'if you cannot see, why do you carry a lamp?'

'I carry this,' he replied, 'so that fools do not stumble against me in the dark.'

This incident has only a slight connection with the story that follows, but I think it provides the right sort of tone and setting. Mr Oliver, an Anglo-Indian teacher, was returning to his school late one night, on the outskirts of the hill station of Shimla. The school was conducted on English public school lines and the boys, most of them from well-to-do Indian families, wore blazers, caps and ties. *Life* magazine, in a feature on India, had once called this school the 'Eton of the East'.

Individuality was not encouraged; they were all destined to become 'leaders of men'.

Mr Oliver had been teaching in the school for several years. Sometimes it seemed like an eternity, for one day followed another with the same monotonous routine. The Shimla bazaar, with its cinemas and restaurants, was about two miles from the school; and Mr Oliver, a bachelor, usually strolled into the town in the evening, returning after dark, when he would take a short-cut through a pine forest.

When there was a strong wind, the pine trees made sad, eerie sounds that kept most people to the main road. But Mr Oliver was not a nervous or imaginative man. He carried a torch and, on the night I write of, its pale gleam—the batteries were running down—moved fitfully over the narrow forest path. When its flickering light fell on the figure of a boy, who was sitting alone on a rock, Mr Oliver stopped. Boys were not supposed to be out of school after 7 p.m., and it was now well past nine.

'What are you doing out here, boy?' asked Mr Oliver sharply, moving closer so that he could recognize the

A FACE IN THE DARK

miscreant. But even as he approached the boy, Mr Oliver sensed that something was wrong. The boy appeared to be crying. His head hung down, he held his face in his hands, and his body shook convulsively. It was a strange, soundless weeping, and Mr Oliver felt distinctly uneasy.

'Well, what's the matter?' he asked, his anger giving way to concern. 'What are you crying for?' The boy would not answer or look up. His body continued to be racked with silent sobbing.

'Come on, boy, you shouldn't be out here at this hour. Tell me the trouble. Look up!'

The boy looked up. He took his hands from his face and looked up at his teacher. The light from Mr Oliver's torch fell on the boy's face—if you could call it a face.

He had no eyes, ears, nose or mouth. It was just a round smooth head—with a school cap on top of it. And that's where the story should end—as indeed it has for several people who have had similar experiences and dropped dead of inexplicable heart attacks. But for Mr Oliver it did not end there.

The torch fell from his trembling hand. He turned and scrambled down the path, running blindly through the trees and calling for help. He was still running towards the school buildings when he saw a lantern swinging in the middle of the path. Mr Oliver had never before been so pleased to see the night watchman. He stumbled up to the watchman, gasping for breath and speaking incoherently.

'What is it, sir?' asked the watchman. 'Has there been an accident? Why are you running?'

'I saw something—something horrible—a boy weeping in the forest—and he had no face!'

'No face, sir?'

'No eyes, nose, mouth—nothing.'

'Do you mean it was like this, sir?' asked the watchman, and raised the lamp to his own face. The watchman had no eyes, no ears, no features at all—not even an eyebrow!

The wind blew the lamp out, and Mr Oliver had his heart attack.

The Whistling Schoolboy

The moon was almost at the full. Bright moonlight flooded the road. But I was stalked by the shadows of the trees, by the crooked oak branches reaching out towards me—some threateningly, others as though they needed companionship.

Once I dreamt that the trees could walk. That on moonlit nights like this they would uproot themselves for a while, visit each other, talk about old times—for they had seen many men and happenings, especially the older ones. And then, before dawn, they would return to the places where they had been condemned to grow. Lonely sentinels of the night. And this was a good night for them to walk. They appeared eager to do so: a restless rustling of leaves, the creaking of branches—these were sounds that came from within them in the silence of the night.

Occasionally other strollers passed me in the dark. It was still quite early, just eight o'clock, and some people were on their way home. Others were walking into town for a taste of the bright lights, shops and restaurants. On the unlit road I could not recognize them. They did not notice me. I was reminded of an old song from my childhood. Softly, I began humming the tune, and soon the words came back to me:

We three,
We're not a crowd;
We're not even company—
My echo,
My shadow,
And me...

I looked down at my shadow, moving silently beside me. We take our shadows for granted, don't we? There they are, the uncomplaining companions of a lifetime, mute and helpless witnesses to our every act of commission or omission. On this bright moonlit night I could not help noticing you, Shadow, and I was sorry that you had to see so much that I was ashamed of; but glad, too, that you were around when I had my small triumphs. And what of my echo? I thought of calling out to see if my call came back to me; but I refrained from doing so, as I did not wish to disturb the perfect stillness of the mountains or the conversations of the trees.

The road wound up the hill and levelled out at the top, where it became a ribbon of moonlight entwined between tall deodars. A flying squirrel glided across the road, leaving one tree for another. A nightjar called. The rest was silence.

The old cemetery loomed up before me. There were many old graves—some large and monumental—and there were a few recent graves too, for the cemetery was still in use. I could see flowers scattered on one of them—a few late dahlias and scarlet salvia. Further on near the boundary wall, part of the cemetery's retaining wall had collapsed in the heavy monsoon rains. Some of the tombstones had come down with the wall. One grave lay exposed. A rotting coffin and a few scattered bones were the only relics of someone who had lived and loved like you and me.

Part of the tombstone lay beside the road, but the lettering had worn away. I am not normally a morbid person, but something made me stoop and pick up a smooth round shard of bone, probably part of a skull.

When my hand closed over it, the bone crumbled into fragments. I let them fall to the grass. Dust to dust. And from somewhere, not too far away, came the sound of someone whistling.

At first I thought it was another late-evening stroller, whistling to himself much as I had been humming my old song. But the whistler approached quite rapidly; the whistling was loud and cheerful. A boy on a bicycle sped past. I had only a glimpse of him, before his cycle went weaving through the shadows on the road.

But he was back again in a few minutes. And this time he stopped a few feet away from me, and gave me a quizzical half-smile. A slim dusky boy of fourteen or fifteen. He wore a school blazer and a yellow scarf. His eyes were pools of liquid moonlight.

'You don't have a bell on your cycle,' I said.

He said nothing, just smiled at me with his head a little to one side. I put out my hand, and I thought he was going to take it. But then, quite suddenly, he was off again, whistling cheerfully though rather tunelessly. A whistling schoolboy. A bit late for him to be out but he seemed an independent sort.

The whistling grew fainter, then faded away altogether. A deep sound-denying silence fell upon the forest. My shadow and I walked home.

Next morning I woke to a different kind of whistling—the song of the thrush outside my window.

It was a wonderful day, the sunshine warm and sensuous, and I longed to be out in the open. But there was work to be done, proofs to be corrected, letters to be written. And it was several days before I could walk to the top of the hill, to that lonely tranquil resting place under the deodars. It seemed to me ironic that those who had the best view of the glistening snow-capped peaks were all buried several feet underground.

Some repair work was going on. The retaining wall of the cemetery was being shored up, but the overseer told me that there was no money to restore the damaged grave. With the help of the chowkidar, I returned the scattered bones to a little hollow under the collapsed masonry, and left some money with him so that he could have the open grave bricked up. The name on the gravestone had worn away, but I could make out a date—20 November 1950—some fifty years ago, but not too long ago as gravestones go.

I found the burial register in the church vestry and turned back the yellowing pages to 1950, when I was just a schoolboy myself. I found the name there—

Michael Dutta, aged fifteen—and the cause of death: road accident.

Well, I could only make guesses. And to turn conjecture into certainty, I would have to find an old resident who might remember the boy or the accident.

There was old Miss Marley at Pine Top. A retired teacher from Woodstock, she had a wonderful memory, and had lived in the hill station for more than half a century.

White-haired and smooth-cheeked, her bright blue eyes full of curiosity, she *gazed* benignly at me through her old-fashioned pince-nez.

'Michael was a charming boy—full of exuberance, always ready to oblige. I had only to mention that I needed a newspaper or an Aspirin, and he'd be off on his bicycle, swooping down these steep roads with great abandon. But these hills roads, with their sudden corners, weren't meant for racing around on a bicycle. They were widening our roads for motor traffic, and a truck was coming uphill, loaded with rubble, when Michael came round a bend and smashed headlong into it. He was rushed to the hospital, and the doctors did their best, but he did not recover consciousness. Of course, you must have seen his grave. That's why you're

THE WHISTLING SCHOOLBOY

here. His parents? They left shortly afterwards. Went abroad, I think…A charming boy, Michael, but just a bit too reckless. You'd have liked him, I think.'

I did not see the phantom bicycle rider again for some time, although I felt his presence on more than one occasion. And when, on a cold winter's evening, I walked past that lonely cemetery, I thought I heard him whistling far away. But he did not manifest himself. Perhaps it was only the echo of a whistle, in communion with my insubstantial shadow.

It was several months before I saw that smiling face again. And then it came at me out of the mist as I was walking home in drenching monsoon rain. I had been to a dinner party at the old community centre, and I was returning home along a very narrow, precipitous path known as the Eyebrow. A storm had been threatening all evening. A heavy mist had settled on the hillside. It was so thick that the light from my torch simply bounced off it. The sky blossomed with sheet lightning and thunder rolled over the mountains. The rain became heavier. I moved forward slowly, carefully, hugging the hillside. There was a clap of thunder, and then I saw him emerge from the mist and stand in my way—the same slim dark youth who had materialized near the cemetery. He did not smile. Instead he put up his hand and waved at me. I hesitated, stood still. The mist lifted a little, and I saw that the path had disappeared. There was a gaping emptiness a few feet in front of me. And then a drop of over a hundred feet to the rocks below.

As I stepped back, clinging to a thorn bush for support, the boy vanished. I stumbled back to the community centre and spent the night on a chair in the library.

I did not see him again.

But weeks later, when I was down with a severe bout of flu, I heard him from my sickbed, whistling beneath my window. *Was he calling to me to join him, I wondered, or was he just trying to reassure me that all was well?* I got out of bed and looked out, but I saw no one. From time to time I heard his whistling; but as I got better, it grew fainter until it ceased altogether.

Fully recovered, I renewed my old walks to the top of the hill. But although I lingered near the cemetery until it grew dark, and paced up and down the deserted road, I did not see or hear the whistler again. I felt lonely, in need of a friend, even if it was only a phantom bicycle rider. But there were only the trees.

And so every evening I walk home in the darkness, singing the old refrain:

We three,
We're not alone,
We're not even company—
My echo,
My shadow,
And me...

Children of India

They pass me every day on their way to school—boys and girls from the surrounding villages and the outskirts of the hill station. There are no school buses plying for these children: they walk.

For many of them, it's a very long walk to school.

Ranbir, who is ten, has to climb the mountain from his village, four miles distant and two thousand feet below the town level. He comes in all weathers wearing the same pair of cheap shoes until they have almost fallen apart.

Ranbir is a cheerful soul. He waves to me whenever he sees me at my window. Sometimes he brings me cucumbers from his father's field. I pay him for the cucumbers; he uses the money for books or for small things needed at home.

Many of the children are like Ranbir—poor, but slightly better off than what their parents were at the same age. They cannot attend the expensive residential and private schools that abound here, but must go to the government-aided schools with only basic facilities. Not many of their parents managed to go to school. They spent their lives working in the fields or delivering milk in the hill station. The lucky ones got into the army. Perhaps Ranbir will do something different when he grows up.

He has yet to see a train but he sees planes flying over the mountains almost every day.

'How far can a plane go?' he asks.

'All over the world,' I tell him. 'Thousands of miles in a day. You can go almost anywhere.'

'I'll go round the world one day,' he vows. 'I'll buy a plane and go everywhere!'

And maybe he will. He has a determined chin and a defiant look in his eye.

The following lines in my journal were put down for my own inspiration or encouragement, but they will do for any determined young person:

We get out of life what we bring to it. There is not a dream which may not come true if we have the energy which determines our own fate. We can always get what we want if we will it intensely enough. So few people succeed greatly because so few people conceive a great end, working towards it without giving up. We all know that the man who works steadily for money gets rich; the man who works day and night for fame or power reaches his goal. And those who work for deeper, more spiritual achievements will find them too. It may come when we no longer have any use for it, but if we have been willing it long enough, it will come!

Up to a few years ago, very few girls in the hills or in the villages of India went to school. They helped in the home until they were old enough to be married, which wasn't very old. But there are now just as many girls as there are boys going to school.

Bindra is something of an extrovert—a confident fourteen year old who chatters away as she hurries down the road with her companions. Her father is a forest guard and knows me quite well. I meet him on my walks through the deodar woods behind Landour. And I had grown used to seeing Bindra almost every day. When she did not put in an appearance for a week, I asked her brother if anything was wrong.

'Oh, nothing,' he says, 'she is helping my mother cut grass. Soon the monsoon will end and the grass will dry up. So we cut it now and store it for the cows in winter.'

'And why aren't you cutting grass too?'

'Oh, I have a cricket match today,' he says, and hurries away to join his teammates. Unlike his sister, he puts pleasure before work!

Cricket, once the game of the elite, has become the game of the masses. On any holiday, in any part of this vast country, groups of boys can be seen making their way to the nearest field, or open patch of land, with bat, ball and any other cricketing gear that they can cobble together. Watching some of them play, I am amazed at the quality of talent, at the finesse with which they bat or bowl. Some of the local teams are as good, if not better, than any from the private schools, where there are better facilities. But the boys from these poor or lower-middle-class families will never get the exposure that is necessary to bring them to the attention of those who select state or national teams. They will never get near enough to the men of influence and power. They must continue to play for the love of the game, or watch their more fortunate heroes' exploits on television.

As winter approaches and the days grow shorter, those children who live far away must quicken their pace in order to get home before dark. Ranbir and his friends find that darkness has fallen before they are halfway home.

'What is the time, uncle?' he asks, as he trudges up the steep road past Ivy Cottage.

One gets used to being called 'uncle' by almost every boy or girl one meets. I wonder how the custom began. Perhaps it has its origins in the folktale about the tiger who refrained from pouncing on you if you called him 'uncle'. Tigers don't eat their relatives! Or do they? The ploy may not work if the tiger happens to be a tigress. Would you call her 'aunty' as she (or your teacher!) descends on you?

It's dark at six and by then, Ranbir likes to be out of the deodar forest and on the open road to the village. The moon and the stars and the village lights are sufficient, but not in the forest, where it is dark even during the day. And the silent flitting of bats and flying foxes, and the eerie hoot of an owl, can be a little disconcerting for the hardiest of children. Once Ranbir and the other boys were chased by a bear.

When he told me about it, I said, 'Well, now we know you can run faster then a bear!'

'Yes, but you have to run downhill when chased by a bear.' He spoke as one having long experience of escaping from bears. 'They run much faster uphill!'

'I'll remember that,' I said, 'thanks for the advice.' And I don't suppose calling a bear 'uncle' would help.

Usually Ranbir has the company of other boys, and they sing most of the way, for loud singing by small boys will silence owls and frighten away the forest demons. One of them plays a flute, and flute music in the mountains is always enchanting.

Not only in the hills, but all over India, children are constantly making their way to and from school, in conditions that range from dust storms in the Rajasthan desert to blizzards in Ladakh and Kashmir. In the larger towns and cities, there are school buses, but in remote rural areas, getting to school can pose a problem.

Most children are more than equal to any obstacles that may arise. Like those youngsters in the Ganjam district of Orissa. In the absence of a bridge, they swim or wade across the Dhanei river everyday in order to reach their school. I have a picture of them in my scrapbook. Holding books or satchels aloft in one hand, they do the breast stroke or dog paddle with the other; or form a chain and help each other across.

Wherever you go in India, you will find children helping out with the family's source of livelihood, whether it be drying fish on the Malabar coast, or gathering saffron buds in Kashmir, or grazing camels or cattle in a village in Rajasthan or Gujarat.

Only the more fortunate can afford to send their children to English medium private or 'public' schools, and those children really are fortunate, for some of these institutions are excellent schools, as good, and often better, than their counterparts in Britain or USA. Whether it's in Ajmer or Bangalore, New Delhi or Chandigarh, Kanpur or Kolkata, the best schools set very high standards. The growth of a prosperous middle-class has led to an ever-increasing demand for quality education. But as private schools proliferate, standards suffer, too, and many parents must settle for the second-rate.

The great majority of our children still attend schools run by the state or municipality. These vary from the good to the bad to the ugly, depending on how they are run and where they are situated. A classroom without windows, or with a roof that lets in the monsoon rain, is not uncommon. Even so, children from different communities learn to live and grow together. Hardship makes brothers of us all.

The census tells us that two in every five of the population is in the age group of five to fifteen. Almost half our population is on the way to school!

And here I stand at my window, watching some of them pass by—boys and girls, big and small, some scruffy, some smart, some mischievous, some serious, but all going somewhere—hopefully towards a better future.

The School among the Pines

1

A leopard, lithe and sinewy, drank at the mountain stream, and then lay down on the grass to bask in the late February sunshine. Its tail twitched occasionally and the animal appeared to be sleeping. At the sound of distant voices it raised its head to listen, then stood up and leapt lightly over the boulders in the stream, disappearing among the trees on the opposite bank.

A minute or two later, three children came walking down the forest path. They were a girl and two boys, and they were singing in their local dialect an old song they had learnt from their grandparents.

Five more miles to go!
We climb through rain and snow.
A river to cross...
A mountain to pass...
Now we've four more miles to go!

Their school satchels looked new, their clothes had been washed and pressed. Their loud and cheerful singing startled a Spotted Forktail. The bird left its favourite rock in the stream and flew down the dark ravine.

'Well, we have only three more miles to go,' said the bigger boy, Prakash, who had been this way hundreds of times. 'But first we have to cross the stream.'

He was a sturdy twelve-year-old with eyes like raspberries and a mop of bushy hair that refused to settle down on his head. The girl and her small brother were taking this path for the first time.

'I'm feeling tired, Bina,' said the little boy.

Bina smiled at him, and Prakash said, 'Don't worry, Sonu, you'll get used to the walk. There's plenty of time.' He glanced at the old watch he'd been given by his grandfather. It needed constant winding. 'We can rest here for five or six minutes.'

They sat down on a smooth boulder and watched the clear water of the shallow stream tumbling downhill. Bina examined the old watch on Prakash's wrist. The glass was badly scratched and she could barely make out the figures on the dial. 'Are you sure it still gives the right time?' she asked.

'Well, it loses five minutes every day, so I put it ten minutes forward at night. That means by morning it's quite accurate! Even our teacher, Mr Mani, asks me for the time. If he doesn't ask, I tell him! The clock in our classroom keeps stopping.'

They removed their shoes and let the cold mountain water run over their feet. Bina was the same age as Prakash. She had pink cheeks, soft brown eyes, and hair that was just beginning to lose its natural curls. Hers was a gentle face, but a determined little chin showed that she could be a strong person. Sonu, her younger brother, was ten. He was a thin boy who had been sickly as a child but was now beginning to fill out. Although he did not look very athletic, he could run like the wind.

Bina had been going to school in her own village of Koli, on the other side of the mountain. But it had been a primary school, finishing at Class Five. Now,

THE SCHOOL AMONG THE PINES

in order to study in the Sixth, she would have to walk several miles every day to Nauti, where there was a high school going up to the Eighth. It had been decided that Sonu would also shift to the new school, to give Bina company. Prakash, their neighbour in Koli, was already a pupil at the Nauti school. His mischievous nature, which sometimes got him into trouble, had resulted in his having to repeat a year.

But this didn't seem to bother him. 'What's the hurry?' he had told his indignant parents. 'You're not sending me to a foreign land when I finish school. And our cows aren't running away, are they?'

'You would prefer to look after the cows, wouldn't you?' asked Bina, as they got up to continue their walk.

'Oh, school's all right. Wait till you see old Mr Mani. He always gets our names mixed up, as well as the subjects he's supposed to be teaching. At out last lesson, instead of maths, he gave us a geography lesson!'

'More fun than maths,' said Bina.

'Yes, but there's a new teacher this year. She's very young, they say, just out of college. I wonder what she'll be like.'

Bina walked faster and Sonu had some trouble keeping up with them. She was excited about the new school and the prospect of different surroundings. She had seldom been outside her own village, with its small school and single ration shop. The day's routine never varied—helping her mother in the fields or with household tasks like fetching water from the spring or cutting grass and fodder for the cattle. Her father, who was a soldier, was away for nine months in the year and Sonu was still too small for the heavier tasks.

As they neared Nauti village, they were joined by other children coming from different directions. Even where there were no major roads, the mountains were full of little lanes and short cuts. Like a game of snakes and ladders, these narrow paths zigzagged around the hills and villages, cutting through fields and crossing narrow ravines until they came together to form a fairly busy road along which mules, cattle and goats joined the throng.

Nauti was a fairly large village, and from here a broader but dustier road started for Tehri. There was a small bus, several trucks and (for part of the way) a road-roller. The road hadn't been completed because the heavy diesel roller couldn't take the steep climb to Nauti. It stood on the roadside half way up the road from Tehri.

THE SCHOOL AMONG THE PINES

Prakash knew almost everyone in the area, and exchanged greetings and gossip with other children as well as with muleteers, bus drivers, milkmen and labourers working on the road. He loved telling everyone the time, even if they weren't interested.

'It's nine o'clock,' he would announce, glancing at his wrist. 'Isn't your bus leaving today?'

'Off with you!' the bus driver would respond, 'I'll leave when I'm ready.'

As the children approached Nauti, the small flat school buildings came into view on the outskirts of the village, fringed with a line of long-leaved pines. A small crowd had assembled on the playing field. Something unusual seemed to have happened. Prakash ran forward to see what it was all about. Bina and Sonu stood aside, waiting in a patch of sunlight near the boundary wall.

Prakash soon came running back to them. He was bubbling over with excitement.

'It's Mr Mani!' he gasped. 'He's disappeared! People are saying a leopard must have carried him off!'

2

Mr Mani wasn't really old. He was about fifty-five and

was expected to retire soon. But for the children, adults over forty seemed ancient! And Mr Mani had always been a bit absent-minded, even as a young man.

He had gone out for his early morning walk, saying he'd be back by eight o'clock, in time to have his breakfast and be ready for class. He wasn't married, but his sister and her husband stayed with him. When it was past nine o'clock his sister presumed he'd stopped at a neighbour's house for breakfast (he loved tucking into other people's breakfast) and that he had gone on to school from there. But when the school bell rang at ten o'clock, and everyone but Mr Mani was present, questions were asked and guesses were made.

No one had seen him return from his walk and enquiries made in the village showed that he had not stopped at anyone's house. For Mr Mani to disappear was puzzling; for him to disappear without his breakfast was extraordinary.

Then a milkman returning from the next village said he had seen a leopard sitting on a rock on the outskirts of the pine forest. There had been talk of a cattle-killer in the valley, of leopards and other animals being displaced by the construction of a dam. But as yet no one had heard of a leopard attacking a man. Could Mr Mani have been its first victim? Someone found a strip of red cloth entangled in a blackberry bush and went running through the village showing it to everyone. Mr Mani had been known to wear red pyjamas. Surely, he had been seized and eaten! But where were his remains? And why had he been in his pyjamas?

Meanwhile, Bina and Sonu and the rest of the children had followed their teachers into the school playground. Feeling a little lost, Bina looked around for Prakash. She found herself facing a dark slender young woman wearing spectacles, who must have been in her early twenties—just a little too old to be another student. She had a kind expressive face and she seemed a little concerned by all that had been happening.

Bina noticed that she had lovely hands; it was obvious that the new teacher hadn't milked cows or worked in the fields!

'You must be new here,' said the teacher, smiling at Bina. 'And is this your little brother?'

'Yes, we've come from Koli village. We were at school there.'

'It's a long walk from Koli. You didn't see any leopards, did you? Well, I'm new too. Are you in the Sixth class?'

'Sonu is in the Third. I'm in the Sixth.'

'Then I'm your new teacher. My name is Tania Ramola. Come along, let's see if we can settle down in our classroom.'

Mr Mani turned up at twelve o'clock, wondering what all the fuss was about. No, he snapped, he had not been attacked by a leopard; and yes, he had lost his pyjamas and would someone kindly return them to him?

'How did you lose your pyjamas, sir?' asked Prakash.

'They were blown off the washing line!' snapped Mr Mani.

After much questioning, Mr Mani admitted that he had gone further than he had intended, and that he had lost his way coming back. He had been a bit upset because the new teacher, a slip of a girl, had been given charge of the Sixth, while he was still with the Fifth, along with that troublesome boy Prakash, who kept on reminding him of the time! The headmaster had explained that as Mr Mani was due to retire at the end of the year, the school did not wish to burden him with a senior class. But Mr Mani looked upon the whole thing as a plot to get rid of him. He glowered at Miss Ramola whenever he passed her. And when she smiled back at him, he looked the other way!

THE SCHOOL AMONG THE PINES

Mr Mani had been getting even more absent-minded of late—putting on his shoes without his socks, wearing his homespun waistcoat inside out, mixing up people's names and, of course, eating other people's lunches and dinners. His sister had made a special mutton broth (*pai*) for the postmaster, who was down with flu and had asked Mr Mani to take it over in a thermos. When the postmaster opened the thermos, he found only a few drops of broth at the bottom—Mr Mani had drunk the rest somewhere along the way.

When sometimes Mr Mani spoke of his coming retirement, it was to describe his plans for the small field he owned just behind the house. Right now, it was full of potatoes, which did not require much looking after; but he had plans for growing dahlias, roses, French beans, and other fruits and flowers.

The next time he visited Tehri, he promised himself, he would buy some dahlia bulbs and rose cuttings. The monsoon season would be a good time to put them down. And meanwhile, his potatoes were still flourishing.

3

Bina enjoyed her first day at the new school. She felt at ease with Miss Ramola, as did most of the boys and girls in her class. Tania Ramola had been to distant towns such as Delhi and Lucknow—places they had only read about—and it was said that she had a brother who was a pilot and flew planes all over the world. Perhaps he'd fly over Nauti some day!

Most of the children had, of course, seen planes flying overhead, but none of them had seen a ship, and only a few had been on a train. Tehri mountain was far from the railway and hundreds of miles from the sea. But they all knew about the big dam that was being built at Tehri, just forty miles away.

Bina, Sonu and Prakash had company for part of the way home, but gradually the other children went off in different directions. Once they had crossed the stream, they were on their own again.

It was a steep climb all the way back to their village. Prakash had a supply of peanuts which he shared with Bina and Sonu, and at a small spring they quenched their thirst.

When they were less than a mile from home, they

met a postman who had finished his round of the villages in the area and was now returning to Nauti.

'Don't waste time along the way,' he told them. 'Try to get home before dark.'

'What's the hurry?' asked Prakash, glancing at his watch. 'It's only five o'clock.'

'There's a leopard around. I saw it this morning, not far from the stream. No one is sure how it got here. So don't take any chances. Get home early.'

'So there really is a leopard,' said Sonu.

They took his advice and walked faster, and Sonu forgot to complain about his aching feet.

They were home well before sunset.

There was a smell of cooking in the air and they were hungry.

'Cabbage and roti,' said Prakash gloomily. 'But I could eat anything today.' He stopped outside his small slate-roofed house, and Bina and Sonu waved him goodbye, then carried on across a couple of ploughed fields until they reached their small stone house.

'Stuffed tomatoes,' said Sonu, sniffing just outside the front door.

'And lemon pickle,' said Bina, who had helped cut, sun and salt the lemons a month previously.

Their mother was lighting the kitchen stove. They greeted her with great hugs and demands for an immediate dinner. She was a good cook who could make even the simplest of dishes taste delicious. Her favourite saying was, 'Homemade *pai* is better than chicken soup in Delhi,' and Bina and Sonu had to agree.

Electricity had yet to reach their village, and they took their meal by the light of a kerosene lamp. After the meal, Sonu settled down to do a little homework, while Bina stepped outside to look at the stars.

Across the fields, someone was playing a flute. *It must be Prakash*, thought Bina. *He always breaks off on the high notes*. But the flute music was simple and appealing, and she began singing softly to herself in the dark.

4

Mr Mani was having trouble with the porcupines. They had been getting into his garden at night and digging up and eating his potatoes. From his bedroom window—left open, now that the mild-April weather had arrived—he could listen to them enjoying the vegetables he had worked hard to grow. Scrunch, scrunch! *Katar,*

katar, as their sharp teeth sliced through the largest and juiciest of potatoes. For Mr Mani it was as though they were biting through his own flesh. And the sound of them digging industriously as they rooted up those healthy, leafy plants, made him tremble with rage and indignation. The unfairness of it all!

Yes, Mr Mani hated porcupines. He prayed for their destruction, their removal from the face of the earth. But, as his friends were quick to point out, 'Bhagwan protected porcupines too,' and in any case you could never see the creatures or catch them, they were completely nocturnal.

Mr Mani got out of bed every night, torch in one hand, a stout stick in the other, but as soon as he stepped into the garden the crunching and digging stopped and he was greeted by the most infuriating of silences. He would grope around in the dark, swinging wildly with the stick, but not a single porcupine was to be seen or heard. As soon as he was back in bed—the sounds would start all over again. Scrunch, scrunch, *katar, katar...*

Mr Mani came to his class tired and dishevelled, with rings beneath his eyes and a permanent frown on his face. It took some time for his pupils to discover the reason for his misery, but when they did, they felt sorry for their teacher and took to discussing ways and means of saving his potatoes from the porcupines.

It was Prakash who came up with the idea of a moat or waterditch. 'Porcupines don't like water,' he said knowledgeably.

'How do you know?' asked one of his friends.

'Throw water on one and see how it runs! They don't like getting their quills wet.'

There was no one who could disprove Prakash's theory, and the class fell in with the idea of building a moat, especially as it meant getting most of the day off.

'Anything to make Mr Mani happy,' said the headmaster, and the rest of the school watched with envy as the pupils of Class Five, armed with spades and shovels collected from all parts of the village, took up their positions around Mr Mani's potato field and began digging a ditch.

By evening the moat was ready, but it was still dry and the porcupines got in again that night and had a great feast.

'At this rate,' said Mr Mani gloomily 'there won't be any potatoes left to save.'

But next day Prakash and the other boys and girls

managed to divert the water from a stream that flowed past the village. They had the satisfaction of watching it flow gently into the ditch. Everyone went home in a good mood. By nightfall, the ditch had overflowed, the potato field was flooded, and Mr Mani found himself trapped inside his house. But Prakash and his friends had won the day. The porcupines stayed away that night!

A month had passed, and wild violets, daisies and buttercups now sprinkled the hill slopes, and on her way to school Bina gathered enough to make a little posy. The bunch of flowers fitted easily into an old ink well. Miss Ramola was delighted to find this little display in the middle of her desk.

'Who put these here?' she asked in surprise.

Bina kept quiet, and the rest of the class smiled secretively. After that, they took turns bringing flowers for the classroom.

On her long walks to school and home again, Bina became aware that April was the month of new leaves. The oak leaves were bright green above and silver beneath, and when they rippled in the breeze they were like clouds of silvery green. The path was strewn with old leaves, dry and crackly. Sonu loved kicking them around.

Clouds of white butterflies floated across the stream. Sonu was chasing a butterfly when he stumbled over something dark and repulsive. He went sprawling on the grass. When he got to his feet, he looked down at the remains of a small animal.

'Bina! Prakash! Come quickly!' he shouted.

It was part of a sheep, killed some days earlier by a much larger animal.

'Only a leopard could have done this,' said Prakash.

'Let's get away, then,' said Sonu. 'It might still be around!'

'No, there's nothing left to eat. The leopard will be hunting elsewhere by now. Perhaps it's moved on to the next valley.'

'Still, I'm frightened,' said Sonu. 'There may be more leopards!'

Bina took him by the hand. 'Leopards don't attack humans!' she said.

'They will, if they get a taste for people!' insisted Prakash.

'Well, this one hasn't attacked any people as yet,' said Bina, although she couldn't be sure. Hadn't there been rumours of a leopard attacking some workers near the dam? But she did not want Sonu to feel afraid, so

THE SCHOOL AMONG THE PINES

she did not mention the story. All she said was, 'It has probably come here because of all the activity near the dam.'

All the same, they hurried home. And for a few days, whenever they reached the stream, they crossed over very quickly, unwilling to linger too long at that lovely spot.

5

A few days later, a school party was on its way to Tehri to see the new dam that was being built.

Miss Ramola had arranged to take her class, and Mr Mani, not wishing to be left out, insisted on taking his class as well. That meant there were about fifty boys and girls taking part in the outing. The little bus could only take thirty. A friendly truck driver agreed to take some children if they were prepared to sit on sacks of potatoes. And Prakash persuaded the owner of the diesel roller to turn it round and head it back to Tehri—with him and a couple of friends up on the driving seat.

Prakash's small group set off at sunrise, as they had to walk some distance in order to reach the stranded road roller. The bus left at 9 a.m. with Miss Ramola and her class, and Mr Mani and some of his pupils. The truck was to follow later.

It was Bina's first visit to a large town and her first bus ride.

The sharp curves along the winding, downhill road made several children feel sick. The bus driver seemed to be in a tearing hurry. He took them along at rolling, rollicking speed, which made Bina feel quite giddy. She rested her head on her arms and refused to look out of the window. Hairpin bends and cliff edges, pine forests and snowcapped peaks, all swept past her, but she felt too ill to want to look at anything. It was just as well—those sudden drops, hundreds of feet to the valley below, were quite frightening. Bina began to wish that she hadn't come—or that she had joined Prakash on the road roller instead!

Miss Ramola and Mr Mani didn't seem to notice the lurching and groaning of the old bus. They had made this journey many times. They were busy arguing about the advantages and disadvantages of large dams—an argument that was to continue on and off for much of the day; sometimes in Hindi, sometimes in English, sometimes in the local dialect!

THE SCHOOL AMONG THE PINES

Meanwhile, Prakash and his friends had reached the roller. The driver hadn't turned up, but they managed to reverse it and get it going in the direction of Tehri. They were soon overtaken by both the bus and the truck but kept moving along at a steady chug. Prakash spotted Bina at the window of the bus and waved cheerfully. She responded feebly.

Bina felt better when the road levelled out near Tehri. As they crossed an old bridge over the wide river, they were startled by a loud bang which made the bus shudder. A cloud of dust rose above the town.

'They're blasting the mountain,' said Miss Ramola.

'End of a mountain,' said Mr Mani mournfully.

While they were drinking cups of tea at the bus stop, waiting for the potato truck and the road roller, Miss Ramola and Mr Mani continued their argument about the dam. Miss Ramola maintained that it would bring electric power and water for irrigation to large areas of the country, including the surrounding area. Mr Mani declared that it was a menace, as it was situated in an earthquake zone. There would be a terrible disaster if the dam burst! Bina found it all very confusing. *And what about the animals in the area*, she wondered. *What would happen to them?*

The argument was becoming quite heated when the potato truck arrived. There was no sign of the road roller, so it was decided that Mr Mani should wait for Prakash and his friends while Miss Ramola's group went ahead.

Some eight or nine miles before Tehri the road roller had broken down, and Prakash and his friends were forced to walk. They had not gone far, however, when a mule train came along—five or six mules that had been delivering sacks of grain in Nauti. A boy rode on the first mule, but the others had no loads.

'Can you give us a ride to Tehri?' called Prakash.

'Make yourselves comfortable,' said the boy.

There were no saddles, only gunny sacks strapped on to the mules with rope. They had a rough but jolly ride down to the Tehri bus stop. None of them had ever ridden mules; but they had saved at least an hour on the road.

Looking around the bus stop for the rest of the party, they could find no one from their school. And Mr Mani, who should have been waiting for them, had vanished.

6

Tania Ramola and her group had taken the steep road to the hill above Tehri. Half an hour's climbing brought them to a little plateau which overlooked the town, the river and the dam site.

The earthworks for the dam were only just coming up, but a wide tunnel had been bored through the mountain to divert the river into another channel. Down below, the old town was still spread out across the valley and from a distance it looked quite charming and picturesque.

'Will the whole town be swallowed up by the waters of the dam?' asked Bina.

'Yes, all of it,' said Miss Ramola. 'The clock tower and the old palace. The long bazaar, and the temples, the schools and the jail, and hundreds of houses, for many miles up the valley. All those people will have to go—thousands of them! Of course, they'll be resettled elsewhere.'

'But the town's been here for hundreds of years,' said Bina. 'They were quite happy without the dam, weren't they?'

'I suppose they were. But the dam isn't just for

them—it's for the millions who live further downstream, across the plains.'

'And it doesn't matter what happens to this place?'

'The local people will be given new homes, somewhere else.' Miss Ramola found herself on the defensive and decided to change the subject. 'Everyone must be hungry. It's time we had our lunch.'

Bina kept quiet. She didn't think the local people would want to go away. And it was a good thing, she mused, that there was only a small stream and not a big river running past her village. To be uprooted like this—a town and hundreds of villages—and put down somewhere on the hot, dusty plains—seemed to her unbearable.

'Well, I'm glad I don't live in Tehri,' she said.

She did not know it, but all the animals and most of the birds had already left the area. The leopard had been among them.

They walked through the colourful, crowded bazaar, where fruit sellers did business beside silversmiths, and pavement vendors sold everything from umbrellas to glass bangles. Sparrows attacked sacks of grain, monkeys made off with bananas, and stray cows and dogs rummaged in refuse bins, but nobody took any notice. Music blared from radios. Buses blew their horns. Sonu bought a whistle to add to the general din, but Miss Ramola told him to put it away. Bina had kept ten rupees aside, and now she used it to buy a cotton head scarf for her mother.

As they were about to enter a small restaurant for a meal, they were joined by Prakash and his companions; but of Mr Mani there was still no sign.

'He must have met one of his relatives,' said Prakash. 'He has relatives everywhere.'

After a simple meal of rice and lentils, they walked the length of the bazaar without seeing Mr Mani. At last, when they were about to give up the search, they saw him emerge from a bylane, a large sack slung over his shoulder.

'Sir, where have you been?' asked Prakash. 'We have been looking for you everywhere.'

On Mr Mani's face was a look of triumph.

'Help me with this bag,' he said breathlessly.

'You've bought more potatoes, sir,' said Prakash.

'Not potatoes, boy. Dahlia bulbs!'

7

It was dark by the time they were all back in Nauti. Mr Mani had refused to be separated from his sack of dahlia bulbs, and had been forced to sit in the back of the truck with Prakash and most of the boys.

Bina did not feel so ill on the return journey. Going uphill was definitely better than going downhill! But by the time the bus reached Nauti it was too late for most of the children to walk back to the more distant villages. The boys were put up in different homes, while the girls were given beds in the school verandah.

The night was warm and still. Large moths fluttered around the single bulb that lit the verandah. Counting moths, Sonu soon fell asleep. But Bina stayed awake for some time, listening to the sounds of the night. A nightjar went *tonk-tonk* in the bushes, and somewhere in the forest an owl hooted softly. The sharp call of a barking deer travelled up the valley, from the direction of the stream. Jackals kept howling. It seemed that there were more of them than ever before.

Bina was not the only one to hear the barking deer. The leopard, stretched full length on a rocky ledge, heard it too. The leopard raised its head and then got up slowly. The deer was its natural prey. But there weren't many left, and that was why the leopard, robbed of its forest by the dam, had taken to attacking dogs and cattle near the villages.

As the cry of the barking deer sounded nearer, the leopard left its lookout point and moved swiftly through the shadows towards the stream.

8

In early June the hills were dry and dusty, and forest fires broke out, destroying shrubs and trees, killing birds and small animals. The resin in the pines made these trees burn more fiercely, and the wind would take sparks from the trees and carry them into the dry grass and leaves, so that new fires would spring up before the old ones had died out. Fortunately, Bina's village was not in the pine belt; the fires did not reach it. But Nauti was surrounded by a fire that raged for three days, and the children had to stay away from school.

And then, towards the end of June, the monsoon rains arrived and there was an end to forest fires. The monsoon lasts three months and the lower Himalayas would be drenched in rain, mist and cloud for the next three months.

The first rain arrived while Bina, Prakash and Sonu were returning home from school. Those first few drops on the dusty path made them cry out with excitement. Then the rain grew heavier and a wonderful aroma rose from the earth.

'The best smell in the world!' exclaimed Bina.

Everything suddenly came to life. The grass, the crops, the trees, the birds. Even the leaves of the trees glistened and looked new.

That first wet weekend, Bina and Sonu helped their mother plant beans, maize and cucumbers. Sometimes, when the rain was very heavy, they had to run indoors. Otherwise they worked in the rain, the soft mud clinging to their bare legs.

Prakash now owned a black dog with one ear up and one ear down. The dog ran around getting in everyone's way, barking at cows, goats, hens and humans, without frightening any of them. Prakash said it was a very clever dog, but no one else seemed to think so. Prakash also said it would protect the village from the leopard, but others said the dog would be the first to be taken—he'd run straight into the jaws of Mr Spots!

In Nauti, Tania Ramola was trying to find a dry spot

in the quarters she'd been given. It was an old building and the roof was leaking in several places. Mugs and buckets were scattered about the floor in order to catch the drip.

Mr Mani had dug up all his potatoes and presented them to the friends and neighbours who had given him lunches and dinners. He was having the time of his life, planting dahlia bulbs all over his garden.

'I'll have a field of many-coloured dahlias!' he announced. 'Just wait till the end of August!'

'Watch out for those porcupines,' warned his sister. 'They eat dahlia bulbs too!'

Mr Mani made an inspection tour of his moat, no longer in flood, and found everything in good order. Prakash had done his job well.

Now, when the children crossed the stream, they found that the water level had risen by about a foot. Small cascades had turned into waterfalls. Ferns had sprung up on the banks. Frogs chanted.

Prakash and his dog dashed across the stream. Bina and Sonu followed more cautiously. The current was much stronger now and the water was almost up to their knees. Once they had crossed the stream, they hurried along the path, anxious not to be caught in a sudden downpour.

By the time they reached school, each of them had two or three leeches clinging to their legs. They had to use salt to remove them. The leeches were the most troublesome part of the rainy season. Even the leopard did not like them. It could not lie in the long grass without getting leeches on its paws and face.

One day, when Bina, Prakash and Sonu were about to cross the stream they heard a low rumble, which grew louder every second. Looking up at the opposite hill, they saw several trees shudder, tilt outwards and begin to fall. Earth and rocks bulged out from the mountain, then came crashing down into the ravine.

'Landslide!' shouted Sonu.

'It's carried away the path,' said Bina. 'Don't go any further.'

There was a tremendous roar as more rocks, trees and bushes fell away and crashed down the hillside.

Prakash's dog, who had gone ahead, came running back, tail between his legs.

They remained rooted to the spot until the rocks had stopped falling and the dust had settled. Birds circled the area, calling wildly. A frightened barking deer ran past them.

'We can't go to school now,' said Prakash. 'There's no way around.'

They turned and trudged home through the gathering mist.

In Koli, Prakash's parents had heard the roar of the landslide. They were setting out in search of the children when they saw them emerge from the mist, waving cheerfully.

9

They had to miss school for another three days, and Bina was afraid they might not be able to take their final exams. Although Prakash was not really troubled at the thought of missing exams, he did not like feeling helpless just because their path had been swept away. So he explored the hillside until he found a goat track going around the mountain. It joined up with another path near Nauti. This made their walk longer by a mile, but Bina did not mind. It was much cooler now that the rains were in full swing.

The only trouble with the new route was that it passed close to the leopard's lair. The animal had made this area its own since being forced to leave the dam area.

One day Prakash's dog ran ahead of them, barking furiously. Then he ran back, whimpering.

'He's always running away from something,' observed Sonu. But a minute later he understood the reason for the dog's fear.

They rounded a bend and Sonu saw the leopard standing in their way. They were struck dumb—too terrified to run. It was a strong, sinewy creature. A low growl rose from its throat. It seemed ready to spring.

They stood perfectly still, afraid to move or say a word. And the leopard must have been equally surprised. It stared at them for a few seconds, then bounded across the path and into the oak forest.

Sonu was shaking. Bina could hear her heart hammering. Prakash could only stammer: 'Did you see the way he sprang? Wasn't he beautiful?'

He forgot to look at his watch for the rest of the day.

A few days later Sonu stopped and pointed to a large outcrop of rock on the next hill.

The leopard stood far above them, outlined against the sky. It looked strong, majestic. Standing beside it were two young cubs.

'Look at those little ones!' exclaimed Sonu.

'So it's a female, not a male,' said Prakash.

'That's why she was killing so often,' said Bina. 'She had to feed her cubs too.'

They remained still for several minutes, gazing up at the leopard and her cubs. The leopard family took no notice of them.

'She knows we are here,' said Prakash, 'but she doesn't care. She knows we won't harm them.'

'We are cubs too!' said Sonu.

'Yes,' said Bina. 'And there's still plenty of space for all of us. Even when the dam is ready there will still be room for leopards and humans.'

10

The school exams were over. The rains were nearly over too. The landslide had been cleared, and Bina, Prakash and Sonu were once again crossing the stream.

There was a chill in the air, for it was the end of September.

Prakash had learnt to play the flute quite well, and he played on the way to school and then again on the way home. As a result he did not look at his watch so often.

One morning they found a small crowd in front of

Mr Mani's house.

'What could have happened?' wondered Bina. 'I hope he hasn't got lost again.'

'Maybe he's sick,' said Sonu.

'Maybe it's the porcupines,' said Prakash.

But it was none of these things.

Mr Mani's first dahlia was in bloom, and half the village had turned out to look at it! It was a huge red double dahlia, so heavy that it had to be supported with sticks. No one had ever seen such a magnificent flower!

Mr Mani was a happy man. And his mood only improved over the coming week, as more and more dahlias flowered—crimson, yellow, purple, mauve, white—button dahlias, pompom dahlias, spotted dahlias, striped dahlias...Mr Mani had them all! A dahlia even turned up on Tania Romola's desk—he got on quite well with her now—and another brightened up the headmaster's study.

A week later, on their way home—it was almost the last day of the school term—Bina, Prakash and Sonu talked about what they might do when they grew up.

'I think I'll become a teacher,' said Bina. 'I'll teach children about animals and birds, and trees and flowers.'

'Better than maths!' said Prakash.

'I'll be a pilot,' said Sonu. 'I want to fly a plane like Miss Ramola's brother.'

'And what about you, Prakash?' asked Bina.

Prakash just smiled and said, 'Maybe I'll be a flute player,' and he put the flute to he lips and played a sweet melody.

'Well, the world needs flute players too,' said Bina, as they fell into step beside him.

The leopard had been stalking a barking deer. She paused when she heard the flute and the voices of the children. Her own young ones were growing quickly, but the girl and the two boys did not look much older.

They had started singing their favourite song again:

Five more miles to go!
We climb through rain and snow.
A river to cross...
A mountain to pass...
Now we've four more miles to go!

The leopard waited until they had passed, before returning to the trail of the barking deer.